THE KIRK OF THE CORRIE

THE KIRK
OF THE CORRIE

by
ISABEL CAMERON

LUTTERWORTH PRESS
LONDON

PRINTED IN GREAT BRITAIN
BY EBENEZER BAYLIS AND SON, LTD., THE
TRINITY PRESS, WORCESTER, AND LONDON

CONTENTS

Chapter 1

THE GLEN CHOOSES A MINISTER

"THIRTY-THREE years of age—thirty-three, ye're telling me! That's champion—that's grand! At that age a man has sense and is steady and knows his own mind. I wonder——" but what Donal wondered is not known, though some of his listeners could guess. "He's merriet, too, that's a blessing—no hope for the old maids, or the young ones either. What like's his wife? She'll no' be a patch on the last one;" and Donal laughed sarcastically and added, "They never are."

The smiddy was full of customers (none of whom were in a hurry), of warmth, and of sociability. It was a time to give and get news. The sharp spring air made the heat of the forge very grateful and the filling of the Glen kirk pulpit was proving a never-ending topic of interest. On this particular evening when Donal Cattanach spoke, the discussion was on the choice of a minister and the reprehensible way the vacancy committee were muddling up their job. Huh! the unofficial smiddy committee could do it much better!—and much more quickly!

Donal was in one of his most joyous moods; he had just put through with great success a business deal not wholly unconnected with a distant whisky still, a moonless spring night and a load of . . . peats, shall we say? Apart from the merely mercenary aspect of the transaction, there was the heart-warming one of "doing the gauger". No wonder Donal was feeling on top of the

7

world, though at the moment he was seated on an ancient wheelbarrow without trams.

Church matters were in the balance just then. Some wished to hear more candidates, and others wished to call the young man they had now heard for two previous Sundays. Their chief objection to this man was that his grandfather, old John Mackay, and uncle had had the meal mills at Lochside, and that he'd been spending his holidays, ever since he was a schoolboy, at Lochside—near enough to Glen Craigan to know all about it. They all knew him fine! In fact, it was the usual case of a prophet having no honour in his (grandfather's) country. Some of them even knew his wife—she had been a school teacher in Edinburgh.

Donal, however, was prepared to give the young man his blessing. In fact, he was in the mood to agree with anyone, even had their choice fallen on one as old as Methuselah. To hear from Dan Gow, the smith, that they were thinking of calling the Rev. Thomas Mackay made Donal utter clamorous congratulations.

Having stated his approval of the young man's age, he fumbled in his pocket for his pipe and viewed thoughtfully its empty bowl. Dan handed him a "fill" of bogey roll, Sandy-the-roadman donated a spunk. They felt Donal deserved well at their hands, for they were unanimous for the young minister: but all in the smiddy that night were not in favour of Tom Mackay. They wished to hear more candidates, and they were determined that the new minister was to be the exact opposite of the last one! Yes, they liked the last one; but changes are lightsome.

Calling a minister is a ticklish job, as everyone knows. Apart from his attainments as a scholar and a preacher, it is necessary to scrutinize his private affairs, financial, matrimonial and social. His physical appearance, too, is important, for if he "speaks with the tongue of men and of angels," and has a squeaky voice and a contemptible presence—*he's no use*.

The present meeting was not the only occasion upon which Donal Cattanach had voiced his feelings. Needless to remark that though he was not on the official vacancy committee, he was vice-president of the smiddy one, and after all *it* carried the day! In the Kirk Committee, the members were tongue-tied—butter would not melt in their mouths; but in the smiddy—huh! as someone said, "The butter would not only melt—it would bile."

Hearing one of these smiddy discussions and hearing of the many excellent qualities expected from the new minister whom they had not as yet found, Donal said dryly, "I'll tell you the very place where you'll find such a man! Only, mind this—you must send him hame at nichts."

This was surely a daft-like proposal. "And what place is that?" Peter Cameron asked suspiciously.

"*Heaven*," was Donal's reply, "for you'll not get him on earth."

It was a much-needed word—for after that the search became less severe; in fact, by the time they had heard their twelfth candidate some of them had forgotten what like the first one was. When they heard the Rev. Thomas Mackay they said, or at least some of them said, "This is the man;" but others, chiefly "nesty bodies", said, "No, we must hear more."

The Rev. Thomas Mackay stood six feet in his socks, and though the psalmist says the Lord has no pleasure in the legs of a man (how did he know anyway?) the congregation has much pleasure in them and like them to be long and straight. The rest of the young man was equally satisfactory, and folk liked his dark hair and brilliant dark eyes which some said were brown and some said were blue. They liked his ringing voice, and the way he laughed, and they heard with much satisfaction that he had been in business first and had saved up enough money to pay his college fees and give him the right to write Reverend before his name and M.A. after it, and they all, young and old, secretly or openly, rejoiced to hear he had been captain of the college shinty team and had won glorious victories and not a few scars in conflict with other teams.

Peter Cameron, the elder, who was generally "agin the Government", now spoke up. He said, "When we're looking for a Prime Minister for our country we get a man well up in years. It's a queer thing that when a congregation's looking for a minister the first thing they ask is: 'Is he a young man?' And I'm telling you, friends, that thirty-three is too young."

Sandy-the-roadman was fit for him though! Said Sandy, "You forget, Peter, that they catch Members of Parliament *young* and keep them learning their trade till they're *old* and fit for being in the Cabinet or being Prime Ministers!"

Sandy Morrison the merchant nodded. "But I doot if a young minister will stop wi' us till he's old. Look see to the way Mr. Arnott went! He said it was a 'call from the Lord', but I'm thinking it was the call o' a city kirk and a bigger stipend. Yes, I agree wi' Peter—thirty-three is too young. I would like a married man wi' a family."

"He has two bairns," Donal interposed.

The atmosphere of the smiddy was inclined to become unfriendly as each man voiced his feelings. It did not help matters that Jamie Thompson, farmer of the Kirkton, now entered, a broken harness chain in his hand, a scowl on his brow.

"Weel, lads, ye seem to be busy," he said, looking around and speaking with biting sarcasm. "When ye have time, smith, ye might mend this chain. Oh, there's nae hurry! Nae doot I'd be glad o' it by the morning, but that would mean ye'd hae tae work the nicht, an' I wadna like tae spile yer crack. Ye'll have a heap o' things tae settle amang ye afore ye all agree on what kin' o' minister ye're tae hae. I can wait—it's no' that important."

Meanwhile, Dan-the-smith had been blowing up the forge and examining the broken chain. "Ye'll get it first thing in the morning," he assured James, who robbed of a grievance looked crosser than ever, and just to mark his disapproval banged the smiddy half-door so fiercely after him it sent smoke smuts into the eyes of the smiddy club.

Sandy-the-roadman who was a homely soul spat into the cooling tank and said he had a good mind to give Jamie one with his shuffle—and crack his head for him.

Again the door opened, and everyone gave a sigh of relief when they saw the gentle face and white head of William Macleod of the High Muir.

We all know but cannot explain how it is that certain people's presence seems to make us uncomfortable, unhappy and speechless, while others by their very presence bring us a sense of comfort, happiness and goodwill. We call these subtle influences mysteries, and in the smiddy that evening the club had an excellent example of this strange thing, because no sooner had William entered than every face brightened at the sight of him. Donal Cattanach rose from his wheelbarrow and made William take the seat of honour, and everyone assured him they were glad to see him, and this was no polite fiction either.

"I met Jamie Thompson," William said in his gentle old voice. "I'm sorry for that man. Since his wife died on him he must be lonely, lonely!"

"He's an old man and growing older every day, and one day he'll be sorry he was so ill-natured," said Dan-the-smith.

"Now, don't be wishing the man any ill," William warned him gently.

"I'm no' wishing him ill. All I say is that I hope he'll be buried in a grave where there is no resurrection."

"How is Johnnie?" the shoemaker asked William. Johnnie was William's little grandson, and a sworn friend of the shoemaker's ever since that wonderful day when he had made a catapult for the young man. It cannot truthfully be said that this brought joy to the hearts of Johnnie's grandparents nor yet to the many cats inhabiting the old byre at the High Muir.

Before he could answer, the beadle spoke. "Johnnie's a little nickum! Didn't he take me fair in the stern wi' a stone out o' his catapult, an' me cleaning a rone pipe in the kirk. Deed, them that gave him the catapult had very little sense!" He thus got even with his controversialists.

"And forbye," the beadle went on, "Johnnie's jooking the school—I saw him myself."

William turned his gentle face on the angry man. "I'm sorry to hear about this, but he wasna jooking the school. He's been at death's door with bronchitis, which turned into ammonia, an' he's only getting better now—the doctor gave him a line to free him from the school."

Every face, even the beadle's, looked sympathetically at William, for Johnnie, despite the fact that he was a "nickum", was a universal favourite. But High Muir is a good way from the clachan, so no one had heard of his illness.

"He's better, and I'm thanking the Lord for it," William went on, "for, for a day or two, we were like to lose the little fellow. He had no pain, only a great weakness, and nothing would rouse him, and *that* was not like Johnnie. You'll never guess who cured him?"

"The doctor leddy, of coorse," said Donal Cattanach triumphantly. "Didn't she cure my own wife when she was ill?"

"Was that the time," Peter-postie asked, "when the leddy doctor cured her wi' an old newspaper and a wooden spoon?"

Donal glared at him angrily. "No, it wasna a wooden spoon—it was a long-handled iron one, an' the *Scotsman*."

The other members of the committee heard this oft-told tale rather impatiently.

"Tell us, William, what cured the little boy?"

"Oh, it was just that young minister, the miller's grandson. He was living with his grandfather at the time, and he was coming every day to see the boy and telling him stories and trying to rouse him, but it was for no use, and at last says he to my wife, 'Have you an empty purn, Mrs. Macleod?' and she brought him one she got from Peter-the-pedlar. 'The very thing,' says he, and whippit out his pocket knife and made *two* tee-totems! Beauties! 'Now, Mrs. Macleod, lend me a tea-tray,' says he, and he put the tray over Johnnies's knees in the bed and set the totems spinning. 'But you cannot spin them, Johnnie,' says he. 'I *can* spin them,' says the bairn, and up he gets on his pillow just to show the young minister that he could spin a totem too. They began to see which of them could spin their totem longest, and it's as sure as you're there didn't our little rascal manage to keep his going the longest? The young minister was fair annoyed, but Johnnie laughed. When the leddy doctor came in in the afternoon she laughed too, and said she was going to write to the peppers aboot the new cure for ammonia—the tee-totem cure."

"See that Johnnie'll no' catch cold," the beadle said warningly. "He shouldna be allowed to sit up in his bed. All the same I'm glad to hear what you've to say about the young minister."

William smiled. "A young man that can please a bairn is to my mind fit to be our minister. Johnnie thinks so too. He's running about the place, and his Granny can hardly keep meat to him."

His hearers brooded over this story. Even those who were not in favour of the young minister began to wonder should they not change their minds.

"And after sitting wi' Johnnie," William went on, "the young minister went east to Betsy at the Burnside and sat a long time with her and 'took the Books' and prayed."

"That was a waste o' time," Peter-postie grumbled, "for Betsy's as deaf as a post." Peter, you see, was most unwilling to be converted to the others' way of thinking. He gave an angry grunt and repeated, "She's as deaf as a post."

William looked at him with a mildly reproving expression. "Yes," he agreed, "Betsy is deaf, but the

Almighty *is not*, and I'm thinking He's hearing and heeding every word spoken to Him."

Again silence fell on the smiddy club, but it was a silence wholly sympathetic, and now wholly of one mind. It was, too, the turning point in this ticklish business of choosing a minister.

When the call was signed it was unanimous.

The next meeting of the (smiddy) vacancy committee was to settle details of a special meeting and presentation. It was expected that the presentation would be made by the wife of William Macleod of the High Muir, whose words in the smiddy that night bore such good fruit. The suggestion came from Donal Cattanach, whose other name is Donald-the-piper.

Time proved that the choice was a good and wise one, and in due course the new manse folk arrived in the Manse of Glen Craigan, and there was a new milestone in the history of the Glen.

Chapter 2

SETTLING DOWN

THE calling of a minister and the placing of him, his family and his furniture take much time and quite a lot of organization, especially the placing of the furniture in the manse.

"Kit, where are you—what are you doing up there? Come down, I want you at once."

The speaker's voice suggested that whatever Kit was doing she was wasting valuable time—his.

He was half-way up the stair by this time.

"I'll come presently, Tom," she said, in the tone of voice one uses to a troublesome child.

"I want to ask you where do you think we should put the wireless—in the dining-room or in the study?"

"I think the kitchen would be the best place," she said; "it's sure to be the usual meeting place for us all. And I'd like it near the sink, for it's near the sink I'll spend most of my time. In the meantime, however, Tom, I must get on with something useful."

"Not at all," Tom cried, in reckless tones. "When one is moving one's house it's always *most* important that the luxury things should go first—the useful ones can follow."

"All very well," she cried, "but when Dr. MacCulloch comes to introduce you to your new congregation on Sunday, he'll probably be all the better of having a comfortable night's rest on Saturday, and I question very much if the Saturday night music would do instead."

16

She had led the way by this time into a bedroom full of half-unpacked furniture and the business end of a wooden bed sprawling on the uncarpeted floor.

She waved a desperate hand towards the confusion, and then glanced timidly at Tom, whose other name was the Reverend Thomas Mackay and the new minister of the Glen kirk. He was known affectionately by his colleagues as "Long Tom". Tom's smile made friends with everyone—just now he smiled at his wife, and there was a twinkle in his eye, for well did he know her blandishments!

"Stand out of my way, lassie," he said, pushing her to one side, which was just what she expected, for she had not had the least intention of tackling the erection of the bed.

"Here, hold that," he commanded, "but really, Kit, I'd like to settle first the luxuries of life; they are the important things—the unimportant ones can come after."

"Like a comfortable bed?" she asked meekly.

"Anyone can erect a bed," he said, and even while he so spoke the end which he had been holding fell with a hollow sound on the floor.

"Anyone can erect a wooden bed," she said, still speaking meekly.

Tom, wearing an aloof expression, pretended he did not hear. Instead, he said, "Don't you remember Mrs. Paterson telling us when she called——"

"Yes, when I was trying to make the supper and put the children to bed and find the hot water bottles. Go on, Tom."

"Well, she said she'd gladly put up the visiting minister if it would save us some trouble."

Kit looked at him and sniffed. "She also suddenly remembered that she might—she *might* have a surprise visit from her brother from London; and—you know how it is?" Kit imitated the accent of Mrs. Paterson so successfully, Tom laughed; and next minute he rebuked her. Nothing daunted, she went on, "Tom, my dear, it never dawned on you that she wasn't offering help. I would say of her she's all cackle and no egg. Isn't that the bottom end you're holding?"

Before he could answer, they were both startled by hearing a heavy footstep in the hall, followed by a man's voice asking: "If you please, are you up the stair? Begging your pardon for making so free, but I did chap, an' got no answer."

The voice belonging to this apology now advanced. Kit could see his deerstalker cap, ornamented with a variety of fishing flies, and beneath the cap the amiable face, wreathed in smiles, belonging to Donal Cattanach, hereditary piper to the Glen and general factotum to its inhabitants.

With the air of a courtier he doffed his cap and bowed, from the waist (trust Donal to behave becomingly). Here was the new minister, and before Peter-postie got in his way he must have first innings!

He pocketed his cap, and from another pocket—and Donal had always a lot of pockets, deep ones, too—he drew out a pair of young rabbits, and still acting like a conjurer he presented them to Kit. "Taking the liberty, if you please, mem, they are young ones, an' tender. Myself cannot be doing with the flavour of old tough rabbits."

To Kit, coming from the crowded city where one bought rabbits and did not inquire as to their age, this news was heart-warming.

Donal looked about him at the confusion. Then he took off his jacket, rolled up his shirt sleeves, and took entire command of the situation.

"Stop you," he said, relieving the minister of the bed end, "if you please, sir, you're holding that outside-in, as you might say, but, see now, you take this end, and hold it steady—it's a beautiful bed. Many's the matt-rass I've putten up when the gents came east to the Lodge there an' John-the-joiner was too busy. Stop you—just a meenut, noo; that's it, that's it—it's not the first bed you've putten up!" he said, at the same time quietly readjusting the sides which the minister had put in the wrong way.

Kit watched the whole proceedings with dancing eyes, and then, greatly relieved, she slipped downstairs carrying the rabbits in her hand, and there at the doorstep stood Peter-the-postie, letters and parcels in his hands. There was no earthly reason why Peter should not have laid down his budget—but didn't he hear the voice of Donal Cattanach mingling with the voice of the minister, and the noise of bed-erecting? And it was Donal who had brought the rabbits for the minister's wife, was it? Aye, and Peter would like to know where did Donal poach them?

"You're busy, mem?" he said politely, his manner implying that he would like to hear particulars of the busy-ness.

Kit, new to the ways of the Glen, told him all her tale, and to it Peter lent an avid ear. By the end of his rounds that day, everyone in the Glen knew that the strange minister who was to preach first Sunday was to stay in the Manse, and so far as he could see the poor man was coming to a place that was no better than a *boorach* (which means wild confusion). Donal Cattanach, of course, the interfering fellow, who poked his nose in under pretence of bringing a present (two small rabbits) had managed to poke his way into the manse, but, wait you, when Peter got hold of the minister, who seemed a sensible chap, he'd tell him to beware of Donal Cattanach!

Meantime, under Donal's masterly hand the various pieces of the bed had been assembled, the mattress placed in the right position, the rest of the furniture arranged in such a way as to allow the carpet to be put down, and Donal saw to it that the underfelt went down first! In fact, the whole room began to look like a bedroom and not like a furniture store.

Kit, coming up to have a look, gave a sigh of sheer satisfaction. "Oh, how splendid!" she cried, "even the carpet laid!"

"Himsel' is real handy," said Donal, which was a handsome compliment from him, for a more ham-handed mortal than Tom Mackay never lived. Tom gave a gratified grin at hearing this praise, which he did not in the least deserve.

"There's really nothing in it—nothing like the difficulty of finding a right place to put the wireless."

"And don't forget Aunt Jane's china cabinet—another most useful thing," Kit reminded him. "Those luxuries are really much more important than a bed to sleep in! Come on down, now, and have your tea."

Donal affected to be bashful—look see, he wasn't dressed, and just look at his "jecket", he murmured, "an' look at the hands o' me," and he spread out a pair of very grimy-looking paws.

Kit said, "Poof, you can wash them in the kitchen sink," and Donal, who had meant all the time to stay, always be here to welcome you, our Lord Himself, who, as His custom was, went every Sabbath day to the Church."

At the church door, everyone shook hands with the new minister and his wife. She, poor thing, was worrying all the time about the roast she had left in the oven, worrying, too, about the jelly which would not set but continued wobbly and watery. Martha again, troubled with much serving. But let it be said in fairness to the Marthas of this world that their men folks would be the first to complain if the dinner was not to their minds.

Possibly it was because of these distracting thoughts that she did not realize that the stout little gentleman in a kilt, accompanied by a tall and elegant lady, was Sir Herbert Higgins, and the elegant lady was his wife. Sir Herbert confessed that coming to church was a novel experience, but there was no doubt about his friendliness, and his eager invitation to come to dine with them or lunch with them—anything that suited—and be introduced to the "young Laird", a podgy little person with a well-nourished appearance and a woeful disposition to suck his thumb—young Sandy, in fact!

There was no time to go into particulars, as everyone wanted to shake hands, and old William of the High Muir, who had had rather a big say in the choice of a minister, called down God's blessings on them both, and though they did not understand a word of it, for he spoke in Gaelic, they understood the gracious meaning and were greatly cheered.

Mrs. Paterson was there, of course, at great pains to impress the newcomers with her importance and influence. She murmured such words as W.R.I. Guild, committees, various committees, but Mrs. John Brandon pushed her aside, oh, quite gently, but quite firmly.

The "leddy doctor" to everyone's regret was not present, having had to fulfil a long-standing engagement with friends in the south.

"I'm looking forward to seeing you and your husband when I return," she wrote, in a gracious little "excuse me" note sent to the new Manse folks, whose two children, Tom and Daisy, already counted themselves old friends in the But-and-Ben, sharing toys and meals with Nookie, and being thoroughly spoiled by Chrissie and old Kirsty, now more or less tied to her fireside chair.

Dr. McCulloch proved himself a most welcome guest. All the same, Kit Mackay was not sorry to bid him farewell, for oh, there were so many things to see to—so many lost articles to retrieve, and above all, there was the necessity to nip in the bud the many plans her husband had as to where to put the gramophone, where the china cabinet should stand, and where was his college group to be hung! Torn between wrath and amusement, she said: "Oh, Tom, can't you find a suitable place for my sewing machine, and did you unpack the pressure cooker, because I simply can't get on without it?"

"Did you look in the hallstand?" he asked in a contrite tone of voice.

"Goodness, no! Among the rugs and scarves? Who on earth would put a pressure cooker there?" All the same, she flew off to examine the hallstand, and returned in triumph holding this important domestic aid to her bosom. Before she could say just what she thought of one who would put a pressure cooker in a hallstand, there was, mercifully for the Reverend Thomas Mackay, a ring at the doorbell. He answered, and there stood smiling and beaming upon him a strange stout woman surrounded with a young family and with a lad in the background. In the road was a car, and these visitors had evidently come by it.

"Perhaps you don't know me," said the woman, "I'm Mrs. Dickson—Agnes Chisholm's sister, you know, one of your old choir girls in St. James's. Aggie said, 'Now, be sure if you're passing the manse at Glen Craigan, call on Mr. and Mrs. Mackay and tell them I was asking for them and sending them my love.' So, of course, I *had* to come. My husband has got a job in the mills at Muir-ton, and we're looking for a house. That's my brother-in-law, he drove us here, and these are my four bairns, Donnie, and Margaret and Aggie and Dick." While she was pouring out this information, Mr. Mackay advanced with beaming face and outstretched hand and invited them all to come in.

"And these are your nice children? Come away in, you'll find us in a mess, but you'll excuse us. This way," and he led them to what was to be by-and-by the manse drawing-room. It was still in a sketchy way, but the carpet and hearth-rug were down, and there were a few chairs. Tom, hospitable soul, invited them to sit down; which they did without further delay, and made it clear they were all needing food and other attentions.

Kit, poor woman, looked with dismay at her visitors. She had not yet got accustomed to the van service, and there was no obliging little shop round the corner to which she could apply in moments of emergency.

"Now, don't put yourselves about for us," said Mrs. Dickson kindly. "If my sister Aggie just knew I was in the Glen and didn't call on you—well——!" Evidently words failed her at the prospect.

25

Kit, trying hard to appear hospitable, was also trying to remember what food she had in her pantry. Well, at any rate, she'd put on the kettle to begin with.

"Just a cuppie in our hands, now, and a piece and jam for the bairns. Oh, Donnie, what do you want? A drink? Milk? Oh, fie for shame, Donnie—in a manse too," and she tried to speak apologetically. Then turning to Mrs. Mackay she said, "I suppose you've plenty of milk, living in the country like this, so, mebbe——?"

Kit, who got her milk supply in bottles, and her supply was never too liberal, filled a mug for Donnie, whereupon the other three all clamoured for milk too.

The minister cut thick slices of bread and loaded each with Kit's last pot of home-made jam. Armed with generous "pieces" he shooed the children into the garden, where their own two children, Tommy and Daisy, were playing with a swing. Not long afterwards the pleasant morning air was rent by sounds of warfare, each child claiming his or her right to the swing. The young brother-in-law came to the rescue and for a little there was a lull in the storm, and during this lull Kit poured out the tea.

"I'll just keep the little chap beside me," quoth the indulgent visitor. "He's cutting a back tooth just now and he's fretty kind. If you could give him a hard biscuit that would be better than a jeely piece. Here, now, baby, sit you down on this nice rug and eat your bikkie till your Mammy drinks her tea." The child may have eaten some of the "bikkie", but he managed to distribute quite a lot of it into Kit's cherished hearth-rug.

The lull was far too short, and presently the sounds of strife arose again. No one noticed little Aggie trotting round the garden filling the front of her frock with the buds of the daffodils and tulips which Kit had been

Chapter 3

THE SOCIAL MEETING

LIFE in the country was, to the new minister, nothing new. He had spent all his school holidays with his grandfather, the miller at Lochside, and in his Varsity days he had worked in the mill, earning sufficient to help with his fees and lodgings in the next session.

But to Kit, his wife, life in the country was an unknown quantity. Her father, a clerk in an insurance company, had been a city man; Kit had been sent to the Queen Street School in Edinburgh and then to the University, where she had met Tom. After graduating with an honours degree in English and History she had married this tall windmill of a young minister, now assistant in the Church of St. James's in Edinburgh. Her background was all of the city, and it is not to be wondered at that she found life in this remote Highland glen very perplexing. The folks in the Glen, too, were equally difficul-to understand. Both she and they approached life from different standpoints.

She unburdened her soul to her home folks in a letter. Here it is:

The Glen Manse,
March 21st.

My dear home folks,

Now that the shouting and the clamour have a little ceased, and before I begin to gather up all the odds and ends lying about, including my wits, I'll try to tell you about the Social Meeting, with its varied programme and the presentations to my husband and myself.

It was held in the village hall, the church being much too small; and to tell the truth, the village one, although it is bigger, is most inconvenient. It is much too far away from the new Camp, and the new Camp is the most important part of the Glen. However, the Vacancy Committee, who really should be called the "Valiant Committee", struggled manfully with all difficulties and overcame them too, so that "an enjoyable time was had by all".

I must say the women of the Guild did wonders in the way of providing tea and cups for the crowd. In one of our Edinburgh kirks, now, this part of the programme would have been handed over to a caterer, but, bless you, the Glen ladies would be horrified at the bare idea! They did murmur among themselves at the difficulty of keeping the tea-urns hot when there was no hall kitchen. That officious woman Mrs. Paterson kept telling everyone how she, in her far-gone youth, kept things hot with a paraffin stove. When that brisk little lady Mrs. Brandon suggested that she should lend the Guild her new stove, the wind veered to the east. Evidently there was some bother about Mrs. Paterson's former paraffin stove.

The hall was gay with spring flowers, donated by the new Laird, who has a gardener from Aberdeen, and that nice helpful man (I told you about him in my last letter) Donal Cattanach played a stirring march outside, a delightful and unusual way of beginning a Church social. But I find everything in the Highlands is done differently from the way we do it in the south. For instance, when the Chairman, better known as Sandy-the-merchant, called on Flora Maclean to "favour us with a song", there was no response. We had just finished 'Old Hundred' and now waited for Flora. The Chairman peered into the crowd and asked, "Where's Flora?" and a quick alert-looking young man known as Jim-the-vanman, with dancing black eyes and a mischievous smile, said, "She's having her tea just now, Sandy, she'll be in in a meenut." He whispered these words confidentially, and the Chairman passed on the news to the rest of us. Sure enough, Flora, brushing the crumbs of her "piece" from her ample bosom, and giving a hitch to her tartan skirt, evidently on the tight side, now mounted the platform. And the amazing thing was, that everyone took all this as a matter of course, and what was funnier still, joined in the chorus of Flora's song with voice and feet.

One couldn't help feeling gay in such an atmosphere, even if Tom and I had to sit in state for three mortal hours perched on the platform for all to see, and I'm sure to compare with their last minister and his wife! But they're a kindly lot of folks, and were out for the night, and determined to wring every bit of enjoyment out of a programme which included a wholly unnecessary number of speakers. There was a minister there, name of MacFarlane, who is evidently in great demand as a "social meeting speaker", a tubby little man with a snub nose and the familiar manners that seem always to accompany such a feature! And didn't he love the applause which greeted his jokes, many of them hoary with old age? "Full well we laughed with counterfeited glee" at all his jokes, even if they were ancient.

There was a weariful number of speeches, interspersed by some really good music, and the electric engineer of the Glen, a Stephen Mitchell who is a music enthusiast, had a splendid programme. A queer other-world-looking lad played on the clarsach and his sister sang. The Laird, his name is Sir Herbert Higgins, made some remarks too, and tried his best to keep his "h's" from escaping, and *then* came the high-light of the Social—the presentations!

Mrs. Macleod, the oldest lady in the church, presented Tom with pulpit gowns, and had to stand on a chair to reach him, which evoked peals of laughter, of course. Then, my dears, *I* was presented with a delightful little portable wireless set, and the gift was handed over to me by one whom everybody likes, Mrs. Brandon. Donal Cattanach, catching my eye, gave me the most knowing nod, and something very like a wink, and then I remembered how he had advised us to put the wireless in the study! You can't help liking folks who take such a friendly, intimate interest in your affairs. And so utterly unlike anything else in my city experience! I have quite a lot of readjustment to do before I can "fit in" to the Glen. Tom, of course, finds no such difficulty, thanks to his early upbringing and his country holidays.

All the congregation know of the many inconveniences of the Manse, but oddly enough not one of them has tried to do anything about it! They sympathise—they agree that it's too bad there are no shelves in the scullery, nor any hot water in the kitchen range, and therefore no hot water in the bathroom.

"Where," I asked in amazement, "did the last minister's wife keep her pots and pans?"

"Oh, just on the floor."

"But there are rats and cockroaches," I said in dismay.

I saw that this outspoken speech of mine was giving offence, and just then Mrs. Paterson, accompanied by an elderly man, joined Tom and me.

"I'd like you to meet my brother Reginald—Captain Reginald Mortimer-Jones," she said, in important tones. "He, like all my menfolk, is an Army man," and with this she left us speculating as to the exact rank of "my brother Reginald".

She, I noticed, was collecting her goods and chattels, including a hot water jug and a somewhat battered-looking teapot. I also noticed that her basket, though it had a lid on it, was full to the top with left-over cakes and sandwiches. I couldn't help thinking of Mrs. Norris and Jane Austen.

Now, dear people, I'll write you later on, and let you

32

know how I get on. Sir Herbert asked me in a very confidential fashion, "What are you doing about your garden?" From his tones I rather think he's going to help us, and won't that be a relief to poor Tom, whose knowledge of gardening is rather less than my own.

What did I wear? My black suit, with my lemon-coloured hat and scarf, my new black gloves and my best nylons. After putting on my new suede shoes, I decided to wear my other pair: the suede looked "worldly"—besides, they are awfully uncomfortable. More anon,

Kit.

Chapter 4

THE HANDY MAN

"I SUPPOSE you're very busy, Tom?"

The voice, like that of the Wonderland lobster, had "a timid and tremulous sound".

The owner of the voice pushed an equally timid head round the study door and looked at the minister bending over his desk and so preoccupied with his writing he could not even lift his head to look at the intruder.

Kit sighed—she also edged her way further into the room. "I know you're very busy with Sunday's sermon," she said, "and I would not bother you, only I'm—stuck. . . ."

On hearing this, he swung round, chair and all, and faced his wife. The dustcap on her curly head had been pushed to a rakish angle over her left ear; on her cheek was a smear of something that looked like blacklead; her face was none too clean, and her expression was that of a poor weak woman. The minister looked, smiled, and then threw down his pen.

"What do you want?" he asked.

"Oh, just to move a mattress."

"For such a charming lady I'd move a mountain—a whole range of them, indeed, including Ben Nevis," he said recklessly.

"Come then, Tom." She led the way upstairs, and it was then he noticed she was carrying a hammer.

"What's the hammer for?"

"To break down Tommy's bed. You know, I've shifted him from the back room into the front bedroom. He wasn't getting near enough sunshine—he'll get lots in the front room, just over the dining-room."

"And the bed——?"

"Oh, I *think* I can manage it myself. Of course, you and Donal Cattanach set it up—the ends were always very stiff—so I thought I'd just break them down with the hammer."

Her husband looked at her with a mixture of amusement and annoyance. "You thought nothing of the sort, madam! You just thought if you beguiled me upstairs I'd fall headlong into the trap and move the bed. But I know you! Keep the hammer, and let me get my bare hands on the bed ends."

No one, no one at all, could have been more surprised than the minister's wife. She even tried to look conscience-stricken—but her dimples betrayed her.

Tom was too busy with his job to notice this. Not without honest pride in his strength he undid the bed ends and supports and marched with them into Tommy's new bedroom—a room which, up to now, had been unoccupied, and was sadly in need of doing up.

Without waiting to be asked, Tom set up the bed, mattress and all, and then looked round the room. "Tommy's lucky to get such a sunny room," he said.

She agreed. "It *is* a nice room. I wonder when it was last papered or painted?" She sighed deeply. "I think if I had a good bucket of distemper I could do the walls myself."

Tom hooted with laughter—incredulous laughter too. Full well he knew that the apparently "poor weak woman" had all her plans already laid. "We'll see," he said, "perhaps some Monday when I'm free I'll do it. Pity we moved the bed in first."

"Oh, Tom, how good of you! Of *course* I'll wait. Will next Monday be too soon?"

He sighed. "I'm writing a paper for the Theological Club on Paul's Epistle to the Romans," he said, "and I'm afraid I'll be too busy all next week."

That should have squashed her flat, you'd think. Not at all! With a mutinous gleam in her eyes she said, "When Paul wrote that letter of his so far as *I* know he sent no explanation with it—he just thought the Romans, having ordinary intelligence, would understand what he meant, but now . . ! I wonder what would Paul have to say if he had to move into a huge unworkable manse like this? His letters would be much more interesting, especially if he'd add a postscript to say, 'Excuse this letter, my wife is spring-cleaning and I've got to distemper the Prophet's chamber'."

"Oh, woman, woman, for a minister's wife you're the most unorthodox person I've ever met. Have you that distemper handy?"

"I *have*—you can get it this very moment."

He sighed as he took off his jacket. "Put a dust sheet over the bed. I'd better get one of your overalls, or something to keep me clean. Or one of my old shirts—have you one handy?"

She produced the garment with such celerity one might almost think she had had it in readiness. "*That* will fit you better than one of my overalls," she smiled.

"Perhaps," he agreed, and went in search of something with which to cover his head. While he so searched, Kit was down the stairs like a flash and up again with a bucket of sunshine-coloured distemper, a paint brush

and a tin of white enamel. She said she'd paint while her
dear Tom did the distempering—meantime she too had
better cover her head with something bigger than the
dustcap.

"An umbrella," he chuckled, dipping the brush into
the distemper and splashing a quite unnecessary amount
of it on the bare floor.

"Perhaps—perhaps I'd better wait a little before I
begin to paint?" she suggested.

"Most assuredly—and you might tell me where you keep
the step-ladder."

Radiantly she cried, "I'll fetch it, Tom. Oh, you *are*
good—no, you're not to carry it upstairs—I'll do that and
let you get on with your job."

"Woman, keep out of my way, and don't be annoying
me further"—thus Tom, lugging the step-ladder upstairs
and settling it in a suitable place.

The "poor weak woman" meantime slipped downstairs.
Half-way down she paused to say, "Bother! That hall
clock is stopped again." He pretended not to hear her.

Innocently she went on, "Donal Cattanach said that
someone he knows—I think Stephen Mitchell—is good at
mending clocks. Do *you* know him? He's an electrician."

"Yes, but not well enough to ask the head engineer of
the Hydro-Electric Scheme to come and mend our old
clock."

She giggled and pretended not to hear her husband
when he asked, "Have you no sense?"

The kitchen clock, a cheap but quite reliable article,
was striking eleven. The sound sent her thoughts back to
her children who at this hour would be having what the
school children call "little play". She had gone some
time before with her two children to introduce them to

their new school. Daisy had attended a kindergarten in Edinburgh, but to Tommy schools and all they stood for were a new experience. Even the fact that he had got a new schoolbag, complete with a jotter and lead pencil and a rubber, did not wholly reassure him. Daisy, being a woman of experience, assumed a "I-know-all-about-it" look which was rather upsetting to her ignorant brother.

The head mistress, her name was Miss Hughine Henderson, was rather an intimidating person with a tall, angular figure. She wore eyeglasses on her jutting-out nose, and her manner was that of a "school marm". She was known at her back as "H.H.".

Kit held out her hand to the lady, who disregarded such unnecessary politeness, and placed a firm hand on Daisy's little head and asked, "What's your name, girlie?"

The child replied, and already she had begun to wonder was the Glen school the same as her Edinburgh kindergarten, where the teacher was her friend.

"How far on is this child?" Miss Henderson asked.

When she was told—and anyone could see she thought poorly of Daisy's scholastic attainments—she turned to Tommy and said, "And have *you* never been to school before? How old are you?"

In apologetic tones, his mother answered for him. "Tommy's five and a few months. He's had a bad attack of whooping cough and is only now beginning to recover."

"Both children will be in the infant room. . . . Miss Gilmour," she called, and a girl who had been distributing jotters and school books among the older children came at the call.

"Take these new scholars into the infant department,"

Chapter 5

THE ANGEL IN DISGUISE

IT was a grey cold morning in the end of March and an east wind had an edge as keen as a razor and a voice like a banshee.

The minister had gone to visit some of his parishioners who lived in the outposts of his parish; the children had gone to school per the favour of an obliging vanman, otherwise they'd have been blown away; so Kit was now left alone to wrestle with a multitude of problems.

The first was a smoky kitchen chimney. Is there any domestic trial equal to the sheer frustration and irritation which a smoky range can bring one? Kit wondered should she let the fire go out altogether, but how was she to get hot water for the washing up of the dishes?—and judging by the soot lying thick on everything there would be quite a lot of washing up to do. It added more misery to her lot that the windows rattled, the doors slammed, and the wind blew beneath the threshold of both front and back doors sending icy cold draughts into the already comfortless house.

Kit, wiping the smoke out of her smarting eyes with a hankie (far from clean) had a bout of sheer despair. Edinburgh! How she longed for it! Why did she ever leave it—or let Tom leave it? Hot water all the time, doors and windows that were silent, gas and electricity and all the amenities of civilization—all these were in

Edinburgh. At that moment an extra blast of east wind, a very hurricane in fact, swept through the house and brought a fresh fall of soot all over the kitchen.

"You *brute*," she said, shaking her fist at the range. The range retorted with another blast. . . ! Only a woman who's been through such an experience will understand Kit's feelings of exasperation. And she could do nothing about it!

The wind lulled for an instant, and in that lull Kit heard a timid knock at the back door. She glanced anxiously into the little mirror which hung by the sink, but things were much too desperate to bother about her appearance. The glance she did get showed her an extremely dirty face with a grimy dustcap and a smear of soot down her nose. With a defiant "*I don't care*" she opened the door.

The March wind did the next thing; it blew in her visitor with a vicious push so that she came up breathlessly bang against the lady of the manse. Both women laughed, and an easier atmosphere was the result.

"I beg your pardon, Mrs. Mackay," began the newcomer, "the wind is so strong it just blew me in. I hope I haven't hurt you?"

"No! And I hope I haven't hurt *you*," Kit said, rubbing an elbow which had somehow come into violent contact with her visitor's big basket.

She led the way into the kitchen. "I'm in an awful mess," she said apologetically, and took a look at her visitor. "Now that I can see you I think you are Mrs. Macnab, aren't you?"

Mrs. Macnab said, "Yes," and she also added, "If you give me your poker I think I could do something about your range."

looking for a head keeper; his old one was so bad with the rheumatics he could do no more stalking."

"Why?" Kit demanded—the town woman was perplexed.

"Well," the countrywoman replied, "a stalker has to lie out among the heather and bracken when the gents are wanting to shoot deer, mebbe even a Royal, and sometimes the stalker has to stay out all night. Then there's foxes and wild cats. Staying out all night they get soaked to the skin. But the Colonel was just as wet; he always went with his keeper."

"I'm glad to hear it—I was just going to ask was *he* bad with rheumatism?" Her tone implied that she hoped he was!

"Yes, he was, then! In the stalker's house there was one room kept for the Colonel where he could change his wet clothes and stockings. The rest of the house was for the stalker—a good house, stone and lime, with a garden and grazing for a cow and 'follower'—that's a cattle beast," she added by way of explanation. . . . "And so we got married," she added with great simplicity. "I think that hot water pipe must be broken, for the water is quite cold."

Kit sighed. "The oven flue is also broken, I think. I've been trying to make a rice pudding for the last two days and it's still uncooked. Go on about yourself and Duncan —I'll try to forget the wicked doings of this range. I suspect it was put in in the days of Victoria."

Mrs. Macnab, after doing all sorts of encouraging things to the range, and all in vain, said, "At least it will boil the kettle." She was determined to look on the bright side of things.

The atmosphere of the kitchen had now become more

and more friendly, and the talk as intimate as if these two women had known each other for years. So in a way they had, for they shared memories of their beloved Edinburgh.

There was something wonderfully reassuring about the way Mrs. Macnab set to work. She worked silently, too, which did not please Kit who wanted to hear more and more news.

"Tell me how you got on when you came to the Glen?"

"It was a long journey from Edinburgh, and we didn't reach Muirton till the afternoon. It was the month of October, and a cold dreich day. The Colonel had sent a gig to take us to our new home, and a gig can be a very cold place on such a day. Murdo, the Colonel's gillie, was looking after things, our driver told us, and he said he was sure to have a good fire and a boiling kettle. That cheered me up. 'Is it far?' I asked the driver, and I could see he didn't want to answer."

"It's hard to be truthful and polite at the same time," Kit intervened. "I expect you really had a long way to go?"

"Yes, yes, much further! And every now and then I'd ask him: 'Have we much further to go?' And Tom Alick Sutherland (that was his name) would say, 'Och, no, just a wee bittie.' I comforted myself with the thought of the good fire and the boiling kettle, but oh, I was cold! On and on we went, past Glen Craigan clachan—past the Church—past Glen Mannie, and when we came to a loch we turned into a side road, and I said, 'Are we nearly there yet?' and Tom Alick said, 'If it was light you could see the lum. I'm wondering if Murdo minded to put on the fires.' It was dark by this time, and we couldn't see the house, but we could hear the dogs in the kennels

46

howling for food. I was frozen stiff, and Duncan had to lift me down, and when he tried the door it was locked, and there was no one there to give us the key. I was in despair. Tom Alick went in search of Murdo—he lived in a bothy near by, and *he* was off at the hind shooting!" She paused. "It took a long time to find him."

"What a dismal homecoming," Kit said.

Mrs. Macnab sighed, "And when they did get the key, the place was in darkness, and I couldn't find either candle, lamp or matches, and the house felt damp, and I said to Duncan, 'Tell the driver to wait—we're going back to Edinburgh.' Well, just at that minute I heard a cow lowing, and I knew by the sound that the poor brute was needing to be milked, and I couldn't leave her till I helped her. But where was everything? Tom Alick found a candle, and Duncan found a milk pail, and I attended to the cow, and Duncan found sticks and peats and lighted the fire. 'We can't go till I feed the dogs,' Duncan said; so when he fed them, and I got warmed, and when Murdo brought in a pail of water and I found a teapot, I thought we might stay till the morning.

"And in the morning the Colonel came. He was a kindly, thoughtful old gentleman, just like his sister. He was sorry, very sorry, for the reception we'd had, and very angry with Murdo for not having things ready for us. He was a homely old gentleman and asked me did I air the bedclothes, and I didn't like to tell him that we were leaving. Well, well, that was twenty-seven years ago, and we are still in the Glen. The house was a good house, not like the brick bungalows we see nowadays. The garden was neglected, but Duncan's father was a gardener, so he soon put it right. And the Glen was very cheery. In the Lodge the Colonel had a lot of shooting gents, and there were W.R.I. meetings, and a dance on Friday night, and a singing school for the youngsters, and a gillies' dance at the end of the season, and so—and so we settled down. . . . There's the smoke again. I have a bittie venison in my basket for your lunch—would it be any use to put it in the oven?"

"Not the least," Kit said in tones of resignation. "It's a good thing the children get dinner in school, and when my husband comes home I'll give him a cup of tea."

"I've brought you a few eggs and a pat of my own butter, perhaps that will help in the meantime."

When this welcome visitor left, followed by Kit's fervent thanks, there was a feeling of hopefulness in the Manse. Perhaps, after a bit, and if Kit got a new kitchen range, she too might settle down, but—not for twenty-seven years. That was a whole lifetime. No! No!

Chapter 6

THE MINISTER ON HIS ROUNDS

"WELL, Kit, to please you, I'll take my mack, but I *will not* take a scarf. I've just been reading in one of your papers that wearing a scarf tends to lead to a double chin."

"What paper did you read that in?" she asked suspiciously.

"Oh, one of yours," he said airily, "I forget the name—'Wood Violets' or some such title. And I decided at once to give up wearing a scarf. You wouldn't like me with a chin in its second edition, would you?"

"I've often wondered," she said thoughtfully, "how a man with *two*, and sometimes *three* chins shaves." Her eyes had the dreamy look her husband knew only too well boded no good for him!

"All right, all right," he said grabbing the offending scarf and bundling it into the pocket of his mack. I suppose your 'Wood Violet' isn't infallible."

The wild March wind which was driving poor Kit almost to distraction in the kitchen was no kinder to her husband. It met him with a howl and made him bend his head. The bone of contention, in other words his mack, he threw over his left shoulder as in the old days his forefathers had thrown their tartan plaids. He still had the long unhurried step bequeathed to him by these same ancestors, and the tall rangy figure and step were what we in Scotland call "the piper's step". Appreciatively he sniffed the air—yes, there was in it the unmistakable tang of heather burning. He sniffed again. Should it be quite so strong? He squared his shoulders and faced the long road to his outposts, for his sparse parish was scattered over a wide area. The wind which buffeted him in the face dealt furiously with the back of a cyclist who, literally blown on the wind, flashed past him.

With a giantic effort the cyclist managed to come to a halt, and then he saw it was the District Nurse, Nurse Grant, breathless and dishevelled.

"I'm so glad to see you, Mr. Mackay—there has been a bad accident up at Corrie Aird. The heather went on fire last night, and the stalkers and beaters have been out ever since trying to get it out. This awful wind is making things worse, and Murdo Mackenzie the gillie and Robbie Ross and Sandy Urquhart have all been burnt. I'm afraid Murdo has been badly hurt. The smoke blinded him, got into his eyes, and poor Murdo, trying to save the nesting birds, especially a capercailzie who was sitting on her eggs, fell over the barbed wire fence. He's in a bad way. I'm off for Dr. Gillespie—Dr. Macleod is attending an urgent case in Ben Loit, so I'm going to ask the lady doctor, she's always so good in an emergency."

"But the lady doctor isn't at home," he told her. "I'm afraid she won't be for some time yet. Could I do anything to help? I did quite a lot of Red Cross work in the war."

"Splendid! You'd be a perfect godsend. Would you mind holding my bike for a minute till I mount—this wind will blow me into the loch."

With a wave of her hand, and a "Thank you very much, Mr. Mackay," she was off, the wind blowing her down the road with malicious fury. It also took this opportunity to tear that much debated mack off the man's shoulders and slap him in the face with it.

What the minister said was in Gaelic, and the historian out of deference to the readers will not translate or repeat it! What he did was to bundle the offending garment into a tight roll and then, remembering the days of his youth when one had to find a "hidey-hole" for such things as a rabbit snare or a fish lure, he hid the bundle securely in the very middle of a thorny whin bush. He marked the spot with a couple of stones; he'd retrieve his property on his homeward journey. Meantime, he'd square his shoulders and exult in his freedom. A fig for Kit and her precautions!

Mercifully for himself, he did not know that Bill the tinker, securely hidden by a bush further up the side of the hill, had been watching the minister. When that be-nighted man was out of sight, Bill crept down and with incredible swiftness hid the mack in his strangely capacious pockets—a hungry and angry ferret was in the other one.

The minister's long stride took him very quickly to the little Camp hospital where he found Matron and her nurses coping with the patients, and thankful for an extra helping hand.

The Matron, who was also Mrs. Stephen Mitchell, was on duty looking cool and efficient in her white uniform. All the same, she gave a very relieved smile when she saw the minister. There was no time for courtesies, so she said, "Our worst case is Murdo Mackenzie," and she led the way to a little private ward where the hurt man lay. He was a sad pathetic-looking object. The fire had burnt off his hair, eyebrows and eyelashes; the barbed

51

wire had torn the skin from cheek to chin, and blood streaked his face.

"Poor chap," the minister thought compassionately, "what a face!"

"His hands and arms are worst. I must cut off his sleeves."

"*I* can do that—just let me have a pair of scissors."

He knelt on the floor, his mouth near enough the ear of the hurt man to whisper little encouraging words as he snipped off the burnt cloth. "I'll try not to hurt you," he whispered. "Would you like a cigarette? When we get your jacket off you'll be much more comfortable." He lit the cigarette, which Murdo bit fiercely.

The slashed sleeves of the burnt jacket showed ugly burns. His right arm from finger to shoulder was one huge angry-looking burn, and the marks of the barbed wire made matters much more painful.

To the minister's great relief Dr Macleod, hastily summoned, now entered and said, "I must go back to Ben Loit—it's life or death—and this wind hinders me." He, too, knelt beside the patient and examined his hurts. "He'll need a stitch or two," he said, touching his cheek.

With deft and skilful fingers, he applied the new salve for burns, one of the latest discoveries in the world of science, and thanks to Sir Herbert Higgins who prided himself on keeping his Camp hospital up-to-date, the new remedies were always available. An injection brought the tortured man a moment of release while his cheek was attended to, and then Dr. Macleod said, "Could you find time to go to see Eppie, Murdo's mother? She's rather an excitable old woman, and if she hears of Murdo's accident she'd at once make up her mind that he's to die! She's living in one of the new houses near the wool factory. Cheer her up! Tell her we're taking the boy to Inverness where he'll get better more quickly than here." He thanked the minister—there was no time for standing on ceremony, and as yet they hardly knew each other.

The hardest thing in a minister's life is to be the bearer of bad news! The very fact that he comes at an unusual hour makes all who meet him anxious. They watch to see what house he enters, and when it is not their own, quite possibly utter a "Thank God".

In the magic way news travels—even in a remote Highland glen—Murdo's mother knew all about the accident. She was an untidy-looking old woman with beady black eyes, and a nut-cracker nose and chin. In a shrill high-set voice she begged the minister ". . . to be coming in, if you please, sir," but already she had made up her mind for the worst.

The minister had great difficulty in reassuring her—it seemed as if she did not wish a single item to be minimized! Murdo would be marred for life, for, look see you, didn't Peter-postie tell her his hands were burnt off? And his face cut—mebbe his eyes hurt, too. "Ow-vow," she wailed, "my poor *truaghan*" (pitiful one).

Sir Herbert Higgins made his welcome appearance at this point, and added his reassurances to Mr. Mackay's. He also promised to take Eppie to Inverness to see for herself that the boy was all right. Why, the head doctor in Inverness would look after him, and what more could she want?

Eppie could want quite a number of things, but just at that moment the minister asked her to thank God the accident was no worse. Murdo's life was spared, Sir Herbert assured her he'd be responsible for any loss of earnings, and every step was to be taken to help her boy and herself.

Both men stood by Eppie's door for a few minutes, and the minister was struck by the way in which all the tenants in River Row kept their little gardens.

"I offer a prize for the best kept garden," Sir Herbert told him. "I want to see the folks in this Glen growing their own fruit and vegetables. They seem to think that turnips and cabbages and potatoes are the only vegetables that will grow. Well, look at the good show of spring onions in Sandy McIvor's garden, and next door Dan Ross is trying out tomatoes." He eyed the efforts of his work people with great satisfaction. "Murdo hasn't done anything to this plot," he remarked. "His mother is much more interested in hens; and hens, as we know, are not good gardeners. Of course, this house should really be occupied by two of my wool workers, the twins Seoras and Ena—you met them at your social meeting."

"I remember! A queer other-world sort of pair."

Sir Herbert nodded. "They live in a little brown hovel up the hill. I've never been able to climb that path, but my wife and Dr. Gillespie often go there. I believe the view is wonderful, and the twins are on friendly terms with ravens and goats and sheep and bees! Their mother was a strange old woman; she died last year. I thought I was doing the twins a good turn when I offered them this house—but Ravens Rock, as they call it, has charms my modern house with its kitchenette, bathroom, h. and c., and all modern conveniences did not possess. Seoras was almost in tears, and Ena was in floods of tears, and they got their beloved 'leddy doctor' to plead their cause with me to leave them in their brown hovel. 'We could never leave our mother's rowan tree and our bees and goats and live in River Row,' they said. They were very very sorry, but would Sir Herbert excuse them?"

Mr. Mackay smiled; how well he knew the feelings of these twins, but how difficult it was for Sir Herbert to do the same.

"I suppose we Highlanders are unpredictable," he said, as he took his way to High Muir and pondered over the age-old problem of the difference between the Celt and the Sassenach.

Johnnie Macleod, now enjoying what one might call "rude health", met him at the gate. "Look at my tee-totems," he said, emptying his pockets. "See to this big one. Grannie used all the thread off the purn to give it to me."

"And she had little to do, you rascal," his Grannie said, coming to the door to see whom Johnnie was speaking to.

"Oh, it's yourself, Mr. Mackay. Welcome, sir. William is in the byre—the cow is not well, and he's trying to help her."

She pushed her husband's elbow chair nearer the fire, and plumped up the cushions. "Run you, Johnnie boy, and tell your Granda the minister's here."

"Couldn't I go out to the byre and help him?" Mr. Mackay suggested, which offer was turned down politely but firmly, with some mysterious reference to a calf.

The cosy kitchen was full of the good scent of fir wood, toasting oat cakes and just a faint tang of peat reek. Merran, William's wife, hospitably swung the kettle on the "swee", and until it would boil she brought out with great secrecy a bottle and a glass, and asked the usual polite Highland question, "Will you taste, sir?" Mr.

Mackay thanked her and said he'd rather wait till she'd made the tea, a reply which pleased her.

"In my young days, the minister used to take his glass like the rest of them," she said, outwardly reproving, but inwardly commending his decision.

By this time, old William had hurried in, and the greeting between him and his visitor was heart-warming. No doubt about the welcome and the response here.

In a Glen where the women were namely for baking, Merran was easily the best. Her oatmeal bannocks were thin, crisp and curly, her flour scones were of incredible lightness, and there were heather honey and country butter. There was, in fact, a feast for the gods.

While Merran was making these preparations, William was asking the minister how he was getting on, and the talk was intimate and friendly.

"Will you ask a blessing?" he said, when the meal was ready.

Mr. Mackay's talk with the old man was stimulating (so was the meal). There were difficulties in the way, of course, but the lions were chained. They were still sitting over the tea-table when Johnnie produced his new big tee-totem. It seemed that he had carried it to school to show to his teacher, and Miss Gilmour had been much impressed by her pupil's cleverness in making the totem. "She's a fine, fine lassie," William said, "and she's learning the scholars to sing Gaelic songs. Sing you one to the minister, Johnnie—that bonnie one, 'The Peat Fire Flame'."

But just then the door opened and Henry Sinclair entered unbidden. He was a tall gaunt old man, with the face of a Viking and the eyes of a fanatic. Henry was always up against things, an embittered cynical old man.

The wonder was that old William Macleod had not managed to influence him! Perhaps he had, but it wasn't visible.

"What nonsense is that you're singing?" he inquired, after a surly greeting to the grown-ups. He fixed his piercing eyes on Johnnie and said, "They're learning you that in the school, are they? Better for your teacher to learn you to read your Bible and to say your Shorter Catechism."

Merran offered him a cup of tea. No, he wasna for tea, it would spile his Scots stomach, just as the foolish things they were learning the bairns in the school were destroying their bodies and their souls. "And now that woman from the south, Paterson's the name that's on her, (Irish likely), she's going aboot the Glen telling everyone that we must get a new hall, one with cloakrooms, kitchens, and"—he paused—"a *stage*! Yes, a stage for play-acting, and a polished floor for dancing!"

Henry was well mounted on his hobby-horse and had it galloping in fine style. Kirk, school, crofts, farms, all came in for scathing criticism, and there was no telling when this diatribe would come to an end, when, mercifully, a shrill whistle rent the air.

"It's Jim-the-vanman," Merran said. "Will you, if you please sir, excuse me, Mr. Mackay? Jim promised to bring me two purns of thread, one white and one black, and Johnnie, you're not to get them this time, mind you!"

Johnnie gave a little gurgle of laughter, while his Grannie picked up the basket of eggs she had ready waiting for the van. She hoped to get as much tea and sugar for her eggs as would keep her supplied for a week. Jim-the-vanman, of course, would probably protest over *his* bad bargain, as he tucked the basket out of sight. Jim did a little trading on his own side, but no one, least of all Sandy Morrison the merchant, who was (nominally at least) Jim's boss, knew anything about this.

When Merran returned, the rain which had been threatening all the afternoon began to fall with ferocious vigour.

"Jim-the-vanman is saying, sir, that if you'll not be offended he'll give you a seat in his van and take you down the Glen."

Looking at the dancing spears of rain, Mr. Mackay thankfully accepted the offer. Jim had been reassuring a group of women who, besides getting their week's groceries, were avid for news of the heather-burning accident, and were not at all pleased when Jim poohpoohed the whole thing.

"They're saying he'll lose the sight of his eyes," one old ghoul said.

"Not him!" Jim assured her airily. "I could wish he would! He always sees me if I try to poach a fish."

Murdo's burnt hands were mere trifles, but his burnt hair!—that was the problem. Till it would grow, no lass would look at him. That was really the worst feature of the whole affair, Jim said, and did he at this point, or did he not, wink slyly at the minister, who was listening to the talk?

But he was respectful and kind, next minute, apologizing for the hardness of the cushions and the lack of space, to all of which the minister paid attention with but half an ear and a very relieved eye, for the rain beat on the windscreen cruelly. When the coast was clear, Jim produced a packet of Players and offered one to the minister (who had, for some time, been trying to cure himself of smoking). Well, well, on this occasion, and in response to such a gesture of hospitality, wasn't it his duty to accept one? Thus did the worthy man dally with his conscience while Jim lighted his cigarette for him.

"By gosh, but the rain is splutter-flanting," Jim said, inhaling luxuriously. "My first smoke since one o'clock."

"That's a queer word, 'splutter-flanting'. Where did you hear it?"

"Noah said it first, when the rain came 'spluttering' down on the Ark and then 'flanted' into the sea. That's how the word came into use." Having thus disposed of the 'brute beasts of facts' Jim stepped on the juice.

As they hurtled along, Jim suddenly put his foot down on the brake and brought his long-suffering van to a stop.

"Hey, Sheila—hey! What are you doing out in all this rain? Are you wet?"

The bedraggled girl he had thus addressed turned startled blue eyes on the speaker. The hood of her navy-blue mackintosh framed as bonnie a face as one could wish to see, but there was no doubt the lass was wet.

"Here, Mr. Mackay, could we make room for Sheila?"

Sheila protested, but not strongly, and Jim, by squeezing over the wheel, and the minister, by squeezing as near the window as he could get, told Sheila to "come up here". She needed no second bidding!

Fortunately, none of the three was stout. Jim insisted on Sheila sitting closer and closer to him (just to give the minister a little more room, of course) and that gentleman listened with amusement to the talk of the young folk. The fierceness of the rain made speaking difficult, but by raising their voices one *could* make the other hear.

Was Sheila going to the Gillies' Ball at Ben Loit? It

was to be a grand affair! A band from Inverness, no less. Refreshments galore, and a floor to dance on as smooth as an ice pond. "You'll be going, Sheila?" Jim asked, giving her a nudge.

She wasn't sure. Ben Loit was a long way off from Glen Craigan, and a girl can't cycle in a ball dress all that long way.

"But you don't need to cycle," Jim said recklessly. "What about going in a motor car?"

Sheila turned the matter over in her mind, then she said, "Norman Matheson did say he could get the loan of a car, but——"

"Norman Matheson!" Jim exploded. "What does he know about driving a motor car? Yon chap can hardly roll a wheelbarrow. *He* would drive you, indeed! Land you in the ditch, Sheila. Come with me, and *I'll* not coup you in the ditch. Sit nearer me, lassie, we're crowding the poor minister."

"I'm enjoying myself very much," said the "poor minister". "I wouldn't have missed this experience for anything."

They were drawing near the manse by this time. Possibly the conversation made him quite forget to retrieve his waterproof. It is questionable if he had thought of the poor garment even once since he last saw it.

When they reached the manse Jim sprang down and opened the door with the grand air of an ambassador. He also brought out from the interior of the van a little exciting-looking basket. "Merran at the High Muir asked me to give you this, sir."

It's supposed that only women are inquisitive. All the same, the minister peeped into the basket and saw a dozen new-laid eggs and a section of heather honey.

It is by these endearing ways a Highlander will establish between himself and his minister a tie that is peculiarly personal and precious beyond all telling, and of which the city minister knows nothing.

Kit had got the study fire blazing, for the evening was raw and cold. The children were in bed, the manse was quiet, warm and happy. Husband and wife exchanged news, while they partook of a thoroughly indigestible but enjoyable meal of tea, fried potatoes and eggs! They looked at Merran's gift of honey and decided to keep it against the day any of them had a sore throat.

"You needn't pretend your throat is sore now, Tom," Kit rebuked, as he coughed loudly.

"I think I've got a cold," he complained.

"No, you have *no* cold, but you've a greedy and base appetite. Weren't you glad I made you carry your waterproof and scarf?"

Tom's face fell. "Y-y-yes," he said hesitatingly.

"Don't say you never put them on? By the way, where did you leave your mack? I'll hang it up in the kitchen."

"Please don't bother," he pleaded, and of course she *did* bother. In a flash she was back, reproach in her eyes and reproof in her voice.

"I can't find them—I think you've lost them."

"Oh, no, they're not lost; I've put them in a safe place in a whin bush, and I'll find them to-morrow." She sniffed incredulously.

Tom showed a regrettable wish to change the conversation. "Jim-the-vanman gave a lift to a girl who was trudging through the rain and going to the village. Jim called her Sheila. Who is she? I can't remember seeing her in church."

Kit looked surprised. "Sheila Thompson. Why, it's her father that has opened the new shop at the other end of the village, and it's reported is taking all the trade from Sandy Morrison. He's Sandy's hated rival. I think it was really sporting of Jim to give Sheila a lift, for she and her father are undermining Sandy's trade."

"She's a bonnie, blue-eyed lassie."

"Yes," Kit said, "Sheila's all right, but Sheila's father doesn't come to our church. He, and I suppose his family, all walk miles and miles to some more orthodox kirk than ours at Polussie. If Sheila and Jim-the-van-man strike up a friendship there will be a series of rows."

Meantime, Bill-the-tinker was having a secret meeting with old Sam Goldstraw in his little back shop in Inverness. Bill said he had *found* the coat—there was no one near it—it might have been thrown away by some wealthy person—it might have lain in that whin bush long enough and so on, and so on. And the scarf! Real wool! Mackay tartan, too. They argy-bargyed for over an hour, and then Bill departed, jingling some coins in his pocket. He deposited a couple of snared rabbits at the butcher's, and in the "houf" which he called his home he deposited his still hungry ferret, and threw him the rabbits' guts, and with the proceeds of the day's outing he got gloriously and royally drunk.

hall for?" Donal bawled. "Haven't we the village one
and the old kirk one, and—and——" A sudden "stound"
of toothache made him pause, and Peter meanly took
advantage of this to remind Donal that when the plan
was first mooted he had been all in favour of it. With
Peter sponsoring it, however, his rage was inarticulate!

"Here's the '*People's Journal*'," Peter said, still speaking in silky accents, "you can see the thing is *onanimous*.
Mistress, I'm smelling your bannocks burning."

"So am I," said poor Beenie, making one more effort
to save her baking.

Peter wasn't done yet. "You should fill your mouth
with whisky—if you have such a thing—and keep it in
your mouth for a little, and then *spit it oot!*"

This was too much for Donal. "Spit it oot?" he roared,
"spit oot the mercies—are you mad?"

"If it's a wisdom tooth, you should get it oot," went on
his tormentor, "though no one ever noticed *your* wisdom,
Donal."

Peter made for the door, not a moment too soon. A
copy of *Every Man His Own Doctor* went hurtling after
him, open at the place where it says, "Toothache, its
causes and cures".

With pretended terror, Peter said, "Wasn't myself
thinking it was the atomic bomb!"

Donal, in a "black-affronted" voice, tried to explain
and apologize to his next visitor, who was the minister.
"That Peter-postie annoyed me, telling me to fill my
mooth wi' whisky an' syne spit it oot."

The minister made no comment on this suggested cure,
instead he said, "Let me have a look at the tooth."

Like most country ministers, he had a fairly good working knowledge of how to deal with ordinary illnesses,

E

though not for a moment would he tell Donal that his toothache was ordinary. "Open your mouth and let me have a look."

The look showed him a very inflamed mouth and a little poke to the jaw showed him that here was an abscess. "You should have it out," he said, "it's the only cure."

Donal, who had faced gaugers, river watchers, excise men and country bobbies without a qualm, got pale at the thought of an extraction!

"Mebbe it'll go off itsel'," he murmured. "Beenie's for to try me wi' a poultage an' a drink from the drovers' well. You put a silver sixpence in it."

Mr. Mackay, being a Highlander himself, did not laugh, at least not out loud. Instead he said, "Water, though it has no silver sixpence, might help you, only let it be cold."

"If the leddy doctor was here, she'd soon cure me," Donal said, and showed symptoms of recalling once more the Saga of the Iron Spoon. "She would tell me too that it's all nonsense about the Glen wanting a new hall. That Peter-postie—him an' his plans!"

"Well, Donal, I agree with Peter. Now that we have so many newcomers we must do something for the strangers in our midst."

Donal, between his toothache and astonishment, could only groan. He also quite forgot that when the plan was first mooted he was in favour of it: now that Peter-postie and his followers (specially that brother of Mrs. Paterson's) were in favour of it, he was furious. "Sassenach!" he spat out.

Mr. Mackay reminded him that some Sassenachs were quite friendly and helpful; there was the Laird, for instance and John Brandon and a lot of the new workers.

Donal sniffed. "The *Boddach-na'-muc* didna like our leddy doctor at first."

"He knows better now," quoth the minister, "and he married a Scotch lassie."

"Aye, an' she learned him how to put on his kilt an' stop takin' sugar in his porridge."

"Perhaps you haven't heard that the lady doctor is back, and I'll tell her as I'm passing the But-and-Ben."

In due course, the lady doctor arrived. For some obscure reason, Donal was wearing a pot-hat; his cheek was swollen and his expression was doleful, not a bit like the usual debonair piper.

He tried to shake off his depression and his hat (which left a very angry red weal on his brow). He offered his chair to the lady, in front of the fire, which she, with an understanding glance at Beenie, politely refused. Instead she begged Donal to sit a little nearer the window and let her have a look at his tooth.

She did not mention that she had already laid on the window sill a little black case containing some wicked-looking little weapons—or should one call them instruments?

"I'll have a look at your mouth presently, but let's have a crack first. You've no idea how glad I am to be home, and I do want to hear all about the Social. Did you play the folks in?" Thus artfully did she create an easy atmosphere.

Donal quite forgot his toothache and joyfully launched into the doings of the past days, and in his capacity as a sennachie his stories lost nothing. He liked the new minister, a nice chap—so was his wife. Hadn't they asked him to help him to erect the beds and lay the carpets, "an' me an' him had oor teas afterwards—Peter-postie didna like that. He tried to get ben wi' them too, giving the manse bairns rides in his mail car."

"But Peter really likes bairns," Dr. Gillespie said, believing in being just where justice was due, and remembering too her own little Nookie's delight when he got a carry in the postie's mail car.

But Donal did not want to hear any good qualities in his arch-enemy's ways and wiles. "We were all missing you at the Social," he said, "and yon Mrs. Paterson takes far too much on herself—a nosey-parker an' so's her brother. And after the Social, she was going aboot saying, 'We must have a new hall—the present one is much too small.'" Donal's mimicking of the lady's English accent was so funny, Grizel laughed, which encouraged Donal to fresh efforts. He described the committee which had been formed, with the Laird, of course, at the head of it. "Trust yon woman!" Donal said bitterly. "Sir Herbert will pay through the nose for the honour!"

"By the way, why were you wearing a hat?" she asked.

Donal looked "blate". "Wasn't Cherlie-the-carrier telling me that a hat cured him—it kept the swelling in his cheek from rising to his head. I haven't worn that hat since I was merriet." He gave the offending article an angry kick. "It's all nonsense to say it cures the swelling."

Dr. Gillespie's eyes twinkled, but she said nothing about this strange remedy. Meantime, she had noiselessly slipped round Donal's chair, and out of that little black case she took, half-concealed by her hand, a sinister-looking little instrument. "I'll just have a look at your mouth, Donal," she said cheerfully, and showed every desire to go on discussing the wicked ways of Peter-postie. "Open wider, please!"

A painful prick—that was a shot of anæsthetic—a wrench, and she held before Donal's amazed eyes the wisdom tooth which had caused him such pain.

"You have a nasty abscess, and the tooth had to come out," she apologized. "Here, rinse your mouth and sit still for a minute. Better now? Of course you're better. I can promise you you'll sleep soundly to-night, the swelling will go down and you can put away your wedding hat till you need it again."

Beenie, rather scared looking, examined the wicked tooth and shook her head. "I'm sure I don't know why the Almighty gave us teeth," she murmured. "They're a bother coming and they're a worse bother going. Poor Donal, is it very painful?"

Donal, feeling his jaw with a gingerly finger, nodded. But already he was feeling better, and his admiration of the leddy doctor had increased, if that were possible. He carefully wrapped up the tooth, and put it in his waistcoat pocket. It would be useful to show in his next story. But he also found in his waistcoat pocket a paper about which Beenie could give no satisfactory explanation.

Chapter 8

A QUIET SABBATH DAY

IT was a quiet Sabbath morning in the month of May, and the spirit of the day seemed to brood over the Glen. A blue sky was reflected in a blue river and loch, and on the hillsides lambs gambolled joyously beside their staid mothers; lapwings with sun shining on their flashing wings swooped and dived and circled, uttering their wistful cry; a lark a mere speck in the sky sang joyously, and on the roof of the manse a company of starlings mimicked and mocked all the other birds and enjoyed doing it too.

The minister on his way to church paused a moment to let the beauties of hill and dale and loch gladden his heart. "This is the day which the Lord hath made, we will rejoice and be glad in it," he murmured.

Like all ministers he liked to have a little spell of quietness before entering the pulpit, and this was the reason he was going ahead of his wife and children: they would follow, but for him there must be a little while for prayer and thought before facing the congregation. He took the river footpath rather than the high road, and just where road and path fork into separate ways a loud cry startled him. Flat on the steep road was a frightened child holding frantically on to an upset pram out of which had fallen a very pretty doll.

Mr. Mackay rushed to the rescue. "Poor lassie," he

belonged to Clydeside, was helping him. Dod was a Catholic, so of course must be excused; and here was a mixed marriage, a bone of contention to young couples, and what was worse, to the young couples' "in-laws", whose feelings ran high at times of births, deaths and marriages. This was another of the minister's problems.

Peter-postie, who was also beadle, met him with an infuriating face. "What keepit you, sir?" he demanded. "You'll be late, and look, see, what yon wild boys have done! Threw a stone through the vestry window! They were playin' fitba' in the churchyaird, and if you only *heard* the words they used to me when I checked them! In my young days, boys were learnt to go to the Sunday school, and no' allowed to play fitba' on the Sabbath day." Then a queer look came over his rugged face. "That wren's nest that was built ablow the window is spiled, an' the wee birdies are a' dead. I could *sort* the wicked hoodlums that did it." He nodded to a pathetic little heap of grass, twigs and feathers which had once been the happy little home of the parent birds, built with loving care. Peter hurried away; words were no use.

All these disturbing elements did not fit Mr. Mackay for his pulpit; no time now for more than a hasty S O S to heaven, and then to face the congregation. It was a depressingly small congregation. True, some of his staunch friends were there; but so were Mrs. Paterson, her husband and brother.

If it is true that the pew makes the pulpit, then the pew that morning certainly did not help the minister. There was no response. He felt as if he were beating the air or speaking into cotton wool which was smothering his voice and choking his words. Stephen Mitchell had elected to go out in his car that morning, and Rob Bain, the baker,

73

who was his substitute, pitched all the tunes either too high or too low, and of course there was no organ. A depressing feeling! The minister's prayer for a "felt sense of God's presence" did not seem to help him, and then he pronounced the benediction.

As the kirk skailed, a charabanc loaded with noisy holidaymakers, shouting and singing, tore up the peace of the Glen, and the smell of petrol polluted the sweet summer air.

As the minister shrugged himself into his coat a voice asked, "Am I intruding?" It was Dr. Gillespie, and full well did she know she was welcome.

"I just want to thank you for your sermon," she said, "for I was feeling very depressed this morning. My husband thought that he might get home a little sooner, if he'd get the workers to hustle a bit. Instead, the Directors have asked him to look up the small sheep station in Australia which Sir Herbert wishes them to take over. Well, well, we must just carry on! I've been thinking about that social service club, you know, and now that you have come we might set it a-going. Your wife and I can get a team any day, and you'll find the young folks in the Glen are all anxious to *do* something."

He smiled ruefully. "Except come to church? They've no time for that."

"No-n-no," she agreed, "but if you get a good choir going you'll find that the girls will come, and of course so will the boys, and if we could get Stephen Mitchell to hold a practice after church, you'd see an improvement in the attendance. Those who wanted to stay to practice must come to church. No one has ever appreciated what a band of bonnie lassies fond of singing can do in the way of church attendance." She gave him a knowing look.

74

her. She's quite out of her own place in the But-and-Ben, but she's devoted to the little boy, or she appears to be. I think she has a sly face—probably knows what side her bread is buttered on."

Kit, who knew and valued Chrissie, said politely, "I don't think Chrissie is sly; she's *shy*, and if she thinks one is not friendly to her she does not show her kinder side. I have always found her most obliging and helpful. If some evenings I have to go out with my husband, she'll 'baby sit' with my children, and I can tell you this there are smiles all round when this happens. And if Chrissie gives them their bath, you should hear the fun they have!"

"If you like, I'll try to get you a boarded-out girl," Mrs. Paterson said, and was rather hurt at Kit's pleasant, but emphatic, *"No thank you!"* But the wind from the beginning of this visit was in the east, oh, decidedly so!

Mrs. Paterson bore no malice, however. Soon after this passage-at-arms she gave her brightest smile, fully conscious of the fact that she was wearing her new hat and scarf. She was also accompanied by a strange lady (I know the word is out of circulation, but "woman" seems very unsuitable).

"My friend, Miss Scott-Baker," Mrs. Paterson said, doing the honours, "just home from India, where she's been working—dear me, Maria, is it ten years?—yes, really ten years! All her relations, like my own friends, are army people." How grand it sounded!

Kit, like Mother Eve, cast an anxious thought at the food. Had she, or had she not, a decent cake? The lovely walnut cake her home folks had sent to her had been carefully locked in the dining-room cupboard, and the key hidden in an empty biscuit barrel. It gave her a

shock, not a very nice one either, to find Daisy and
Tommy each armed with a generous slice, while Tommy,
putting the key into the biscuit barrel, asked, with his
mouth full to bursting, "Isn't it here you keep the key,
Mummy?" Both children were so honestly pleased with
themselves, she had not the courage to scold them. In-
cidentally, she never again tried to hide an extra good
cake! Well, there was nothing for it but to produce the
home-made gingerbread.

"Have you ever been in India?" Miss Scott-Baker's
voice was low and deep; her face registered strong disapproval, too! A minister's wife had no business to wear
such a frivolous-looking blouse—it was bad for the congregation. She herself always wore a plain shirt blouse
with a collar and tie. Her hat had a "none-of-your-non-
sense" air about it—plain brown felt with a plain brown
ribbon, and below a plain brown face and a pair of very
unfriendly brown eyes. Her skirt was of thick tweed and
so short that when she sat down it did unkind things to
her legs. Doubtless she was wise, coming from a warm
country, to wear woollen stockings and low-heeled, sensible shoes. Kit, whose footwear was neither woollen nor
sensible, tucked her feet below her chair. Afterwards,
recounting her experiences to her husband, she said,
"She looked the very picture of a *woman with a mission*.
No one need blame the heathen for raging, if they have to
put up with the like of Miss Maria Scott-Baker, even if
her people are all superior army people."

"Miss Scott-Baker has very kindly promised to address
our Guild," Mrs. Paterson said, as one who brings good
tidings. "I've tried to get hold of Mrs. MacGlashan, but
you know she isn't really suitable for a President. She
was"—here Mrs. Paterson lowered her voice mysteriously

—"she was a housemaid in Scatwell Castle, and you know . . ."

No, Kit didn't know (neither did she care). She liked Mrs. MacGlashan.

Mrs. Paterson went on: "You are the proper person for this office, and I propose to bring your name up at our next meeting, when we can make our final arrangements about Miss Scott-Baker's visit. I wonder, now, if Dr. Gillespie could arrange to drive my friend back to Muirton? She came up to-day with a mutual friend who had to return to town at once. I must see about this! There's so many things to see about, but *all*"—here she smiled brightly—"all so very much worth while when we get a speaker like my dear old friend, Maria Scott-Baker."

The lady thus referred to bridled and looked coy. She had an alarming way of giving a sudden laugh and just as suddenly stopping in the middle of it.

She drank three cups of tea and ate a thick slice of gingerbread, "I feel like a schoolboy with a tuck box," she exclaimed, helping herself to a second slice and following both with a biscuit.

Mrs. Paterson, who had a one-track mind, was still thinking over the promised visit; one or two points had still to be cleared up. As it was to be the opening meeting, the Guild must provide tea and cakes. She was willing to bring some of her own china cups, and a silver teapot—she supposed the other members could supply the other necessary things, such as tea, sugar, milk, sandwiches, buns. Leaving nothing to chance, she asked Kit if the Guild could depend upon her for a dozen-and-a-half small cakes.

Kit promised, fervently hoping that her temperamental oven would "oblige" that day.

Miss Maria Scott-Baker said she had a message—a message which all Scotland must hear. She found a deplorable ignorance among her countrymen and countrywomen as to the true state of missions in India. She eyed Kit sternly at this point, and that poor woman feeling abashed said, "In our last church my class of girls dressed dolls to send to an Indian school. They took a great deal of trouble to dress them, according to the mission orders."

"Ah, yes! A little thing like that arouses interest. Did your class carry on?"

"No, for we never heard a word about the dolls—not even a thank-you postcard, and when I asked the girls next year they said they'd rather dress dolls for a babies' home in Edinburgh. Edinburgh was my last home," she added a little wistfully.

"Of course, Miss Maria Scott-Baker will stay overnight," Mrs. Paterson went on, fixing her friend with her eye, and going on to say, "Maria, you will be very comfortable in the manse, won't you?"

"I'm sure I shall," replied the lady, with an almost gracious nod of her head. "I've become quite careless of my creature comforts, so to speak. I can put up with anything."

Kit gasped; she certainly had not expected to extend hospitality to an unbidden guest, even to one as condescending as Miss Maria Scott-Baker. She gave an untruthful and reluctant, "I'll be very pleased," and hoped Heaven would forgive her. After all, wasn't it St. Paul who exhorted people to show hospitality without grudging, and hadn't he been quick enough to accept the hospitality of Lydia, the seller of purple? History is silent as to whether her beds and chairs were comfortable or not; or

"Here we are," Mrs. Paterson cried, "bright and early. I want to go into this business thoroughly, and so do our President and Secretary."

Mrs. MacGlashan and Ina Douglas, the two officials, looked thoroughly uncomfortable; it would have needed a double amount of Mrs. Paterson's "brass neck" to relieve an embarrassing situation for them, and how deeply sorry they were they had not attended to the manse repairs while it was empty!

"I've just been telling these two ladies," Mrs. Paterson said, "that the minister can't be taking any interest in his garden—the naughty man! Tell him to take half-an-hour there every morning and he'll feel better in every way. That rose tree, excuse me, is needing richer soil and more—much more—water." She poked a determined finger into the soil. "Bone dry," she announced. Then she turned to the others. "Needs feeding," she said.

Mrs. MacGlashan murmured something about farmyard manure being good for roses.

"Have you any? Well, when you're bringing some to the manse do remember to leave a bucketful at my house. You know, of course, you can't make a rose blush—no matter how much you feed it!" And with this pleasant item of rose culture she made straight for the kitchen.

But Kit, smiling but quite firm, said, "This way, please," and opened the drawing-room door. "Please sit down—I see Mrs. Brandon and Dr. Gillespie coming," and Kit went to welcome her next guests.

But Mrs. Paterson had no intention of sitting down; instead she took up a critical position in the middle of the floor. "Quite a nice little lounge," she said, speaking in a peculiar hissing whisper. "I see our hostess is going to give us tea." She nodded at Kit's dainty little tea-table.

"Rather pretty china," she said. "I've a very old set of real Dresden—of course, these are quite a good imitation."

The entrance of the newcomers put a stop to her further revelations.

Mrs. Brandon, looking more like a mischievous squirrel than ever, was wearing a most becoming new hat (most unsuitable for one in her position). But did she mind what Mrs. Paterson thought? Not she! She knew, her husband, the mirror and the lady doctor had all told her, she looked charming! And there was no doubt in the minds of others that her naughty head was full of plans to annoy the lady whom at her back she profanely called "Mrs. Importance".

"I've just had a note from Lady Gray, our Honorary President, regretting that she cannot be here to-day," Mrs. MacGlashan said. Turning to Mrs. Paterson she added, "I've just had a letter from our last minister's wife, too—she still takes a great interest in the Glen. You remember her aunt, a daughter of Sir Donald Macnab, a big noise in the shipping world. . . ?"

"Of *course* I remember Molly Dunlop—a dear friend! She's just gone to Canada—I hear from her regularly."

"You can't have heard from her *recently*," Sheila Brandon said in silky tones, "for she's gone to Malaya—she has a great interest in the work there."

"Can I help you with the tea?" asked the lady doctor, who found the atmosphere was decidedly cool.

The district nurse and Alison Gilmour, the young teacher, were the next arrivals, and when they had found seats Kit thankfully retired to the kitchen, where the lady doctor and Mrs. MacGlashan both joined her. Mrs. MacGlashan was carrying an intriguing-looking bag. "I've brought you a few cream scones," she said, "I hope

It was a signal for all the others to take their departure, and with many handshakings and warm thanks they went on their way. In a moment Mrs. Paterson was back. "I noticed the crusts of bread and meat, Mrs Mackay. Do you mind if I take them home for my hens? I keep a few fowls, just to supply our own breakfast table and have a few fresh eggs to give to a sick friend! Have you a little bag? Oh, thank you, but that's a shopping bag—do you want it back? No? Well, thank you—good-bye once more. I must remember to bring you a few fresh eggs," which was, from Mrs. Paterson, a pious fib.

By breathless exertions she overtook the other members of the deputation. After the manner of committees, they were having a second and more outspoken meeting. On one point they all agreed—that something must be done, and at once. The money question would arise, but, "We'll make it a nice manse," said Ina Douglas, who after her private conversation *re* plovers' eggs had conceived a warm regard for the minister's wife.

"We should like to make the manse comfortable for poor Mrs. Mackay," said Mrs. Paterson, and immediately Sheila Brandon took up the cudgels.

"I don't know why every congregation insists on it that if they do anything for the manse the minister's wife should receive it with personal gratitude! It's *not* for the minister's wife—it's for the congregation."

"We had quite a nice afternoon," said Mrs. Paterson, "and Mrs. Mackay is really quite a nice little woman, but I'm afraid she's not a very thrifty woman, or a good manager. All those crusts and crumbs left on the kitchen table! Why, she should have made them into a bread pudding for her children's dinner."

95

The district nurse, who was an outsider in the Glen, could speak her own mind. "It's a good thing she didn't keep the bread and crusts for a bread pudding. It would have been a loss for your hens!"

Mrs. Paterson affected to think this was a joke. "We must consider how to raise money for all these improvements. But my brother Reginald has been in communication with some of the Hydro-Electric managers and they have all agreed that with the increasing population of the Glen they really must have a new hall. The present one is an inconvenient place and much too small."

The various ways of raising money occupied the committee all their way home, and doubtless occupied their menfolk too, and the result of all these thoughts must go into another chapter.

Chapter 11

JAMES STEWART, TINKER

WHILE Kate interviewed her deputation of women folk, Tom, very wisely, announced that he was going to pay a visit to the tinkers' camp where an old tinker was lying very ill, and had asked to see the minister.

From time immemorial, tinkers had been allowed to camp on a veritable No Man's Land, a piece of ground where the Torran and the Black Burn met, an ideal spot, a very paradise for poachers. But no one could say a word about it—the rights had been granted to the tribe and taken full advantage of since pre-Reformation times.

The manse folks had heard about the old tinker's illness from his grandson Hughie, a red-headed, bare-legged little beggar if ever there was one! He called daily at the manse back door, begging for "a puckle tea, a grainie sugar, a twa-three tatties," and one day, for a "hair comb"! It was then he told them of his granda's illness—he hadn't been able to go with the rest of the clan who had travelled to Cromarty, leaving "my grannie" and Hughie in charge. His granda wanted to see the minister, Hughie repeated. . . . So the minister concluded that the day of the visit of the deputation would suit him for this visit—it just so happened, Tom hadn't planned it, oh, no! The camp was miles up the Glen, and Tom concluded that the very last of the women's deputation would have gone by the time he returned home.

He found old James Stewart lying on a bed of straw,

sheltered from the wind by an upturned cart, while an ancient and starved looking horse tethered to a post cropped the grass with hungry eagerness. A fire of green wood sent out a pungent smell into the air, a three-legged pot swung over the flames, and old Nelldie, James's wife, crouched on her hunkers feeding the flames with bunches of dry whin.

Much visiting of sick folks had taught the minister a lot about illness, and he knew at once that James Stewart was a very sick man. The flushed face, the fever-bright eyes, the hurried breathing all spoke of some wasting trouble. . . . Yes, she said, he had had a cauld. She had given him a dose of honey, and of this—("this" was a decoction of melted snails)—she had put sphagnum moss on his breast where the pain was worst, she had given him a boiling of herbs to make him sleep; but the cough wouldn't let him sleep, "and, look see"—she lowered her voice—"when Jeemie coughs he spits, blood——"

"You must get a doctor," the minister urged them, but both the old couple said, "No"—they didn't like doctors. It seemed difficult to help them, and the prayer the minister offered was a prayer for guidance.

On his way home, Tom, on his far-from-young bicycle, met Dr. Gillespie in her car, and with one accord both stopped to exchange news.

"Could you visit a patient who doesn't believe in doctors, but who is urgently needing a doctor?" he asked, and went on to tell of James Stewart's illness.

"How do you get to the tinkers' camp? I've never been there."

"There's an old road—you can hardly see it now—called 'The Monks' Road'; there must have been a monastery, or maybe a chapel, in the old days. The airmen from the aerodrome were the first to spot the foundations of what looked like a church or chapel, and to the west is an old burying ground called, in Gaelic, 'The field of the graves'."

It all sounded so interesting, and the invalid's state so urgent, that Dr. Gillespie urged the minister to hide his bicycle and to accompany her to the camp.

Both Jamie and his wife were pleased to see the minister again, and he explained that he had brought a lady with him who might, perhaps, help Jamie. Neither husband nor wife appeared grateful.

"Is she a spaewife?" Nelldie asked suspiciously.

Dr. Gillespie answered, "Yes, that's just what I am. Would your husband be better inside the tent?"

"Jamie likes the wind on his face," Nelldie answered, echoing another gipsy's words about "the wind on the heath".

Dr. Gillespie knelt on the ground, and when she took out of her black bag a stethoscope both tinkers regarded her suspiciously. Jamie's pulse was racing, his temperature (which she took with much difficulty) was over 103, and the tearing cough was, too often, tinged with red.

"Could you get me some hot water?" the doctor asked.

"What for?" Nelldie was still suspicious.

"I would try to steam your husband's throat—it would help his cough."

Nelldie told her that she had her own cures and had tried them.

"Let me try mine," Dr. Gillespie urged.

All the appliances here were primitive, but both minister and doctor worked in harmony, and the sick man' breathing did grow a little easier; "M. & B.", that blessed drug, reduced his temperature. Both doctor and minister promised to come back next day.

As doctor and minister went home, Mr. Mackay told of this tinker who was really the last of our itinerant *ceard airgid*, that is, a silversmith.

Dr. Grizel said, "I had noticed the man's hands when I felt his pulse, brown as berries, but with long clever-looking fingers; the skilful hands of a craftsman."

"I got his story from his wife," Mr. Mackay said. "She told me that Jamie had inherited his craft from his father, who had got it from his father, and so on till we come to Culloden and the proscribing of the Highland dress. For thirty-five years, no Highlander could wear his national dress, and when the ban was raised, kilts, long hidden away, came to light again, but the lovely ornaments had had to be sold to buy bread, for that last battle of ours had drained our country of men and of money. It was then the Clan Stewart came into their own. Shemus Stewart from Oban offered to buy from any hard-up lady her silver platter, her cherished teapot, her candlesticks, and sitting by the kitchen fire he'd melt these articles down, and with the tools belonging to a silversmith he'd fashion bonnet brooches, shoulder pins, targes, buckles for the brogues, and from the old lapidary in Oban and from one in Inverness he'd embellish these ornaments and make them things of barbaric beauty."

"Why," Dr. Gillespie said, "I have a plaid pin—Miss Brodie gave it to me. But what a thrill it is to hear how it all came about!"

"And what a pity Jamie didn't teach some of the younger men here his wonderful craftsmanship."

As they parted, Dr. Gillespie said, "I'm afraid Jamie's days are numbered, Mr. Mackay. His heart is just worn out. I wonder could we persuade him to go to the hospital? An oxygen tent would help."

But poor Jamie did not need anything they could do for him. His poor lonely old wife said to one of her clan who had arrived: "Tell the minister and the spaewife that Jamie died, and before he went a-travelling he said, 'Thank you'. Tell them they both helped him, and he said, 'God bless you both!' "

"The auld man passed awa' at day-set. The liftin' is on Friday at two o'clock, an' the auld wife wants you and the spaewife tae come."

The speaker was James Stewart, oldest son of the dead man, and his words were addressed to the minister, and almost amounted to a royal command. Hiding behind the tinker was Hughie, who now came forward with a whine and said, "Wife, gie's a piece—sure's death I hadna a bite since gitcher (grandfather) died."

Kit, to whom he made this request, looked at him with a twinkle in her eye. Up till now, she had always granted him his requests. She said, "Why don't you eat the big biscuit that's sticking out of your pocket? You can't be hungry."

Hughie, the incomparable little liar, gave a pat to that betraying bulge in his pocket and said, "That's for wee Jamie. I'm keeping it for the bairn." As the bairn was about three weeks old, Kit laughed incredulously. All the same, she gave the little rascal a jelly piece.

Mr. Mackay agreed to be present, and agreed to let the spaewife know.

The tinkers had spread their news in their queer way, and a crowd of men, women, children and dogs were already at the camp when Mr. Mackay and Dr. Gillespie arrived. They very wisely hid their car beneath an over-hanging bank, and made their way to the little tent in which James Stewart had been born and in which he had died.

This was James Stewart's day. He lay in an open coffin, and was cleaner and better clad than he had ever been in the days of his flesh. A plate of salt was on his breast, a cross of rowan twigs was laid on his head, and a green sod was beneath his feet. There was about the man a dignity and a majesty which influenced all around him and hushed every voice.

Never had Mr. Mackay a more attentive or a more receptive congregation than he had that sunny June day. The men listened with bared and bowed heads, the women, an anxious eye on the weans, followed every word, and some of them were in tears.

From the Torran and the burn came the soft murmur of the waters as they travelled seaward; the hush and spell of the unseen were potent; the old hills looked down serenely—a poor mortal had gone a-travelling, while they remained immovable.

"I am the Resurrection and the Life," the minister read, and wondered what these strange words meant to the tinker folk. "He that believeth in Me . . ."

After the little service, the coffin was closed and lifted on to the cart. Then the mourners formed a procession, rather a raggle-taggle one, and went stringing up the Corrie.

Jamie the tinker, the dead man's older son, with some rather pathetic desire to behave like "fowk", walked beside the minister; the spaewife could come with the other women. The one thought common to them all was this mystery of death—otherwise oceans divided them.

'gitcher' for grandfather is new, and so is the distinction between 'tinker' and 'fowk'. A queer, dark, pagan page in our country's history," she said, with a little shiver. "What are we doing to help them?"

The car had jolted its way over the bumpy ground and now they were in sight of Loch Craigan. "Oh, look!" she cried, "the swans have come back."

"Were they ever away?"

"Yes, while that huge dam at Loch-na-Mulloch was made. I'm so glad they are back."

"Yes, and I see they have brought their family," Mr. Mackay said, pointing to a little gay flotilla of cygnets following in their parents' wake.

Grizel looked, and judging by her face she liked looking! "I wonder do the roe-deer come again? They used to come to this loch to drink. It was in this loch I caught my first salmon!"

"Well, if you look closely at that clump of alders to the left of the bank, you'll see someone that looks very like a fisher—and if that's not Hamish Breabadair, I'm sorely mistaken! The rascal!"

Grizel cried happily, "Yes, yes, that's just Hamish. He and my husband—he wasn't my husband then—helped me to land a huge salmon. I forget its weight now, but it was enormous."

"Of course it was," the minister agreed with suspicious alacrity.

"We had a dog too—Beauty—a lovely black cocker spaniel," she sighed, as she waved farewell to all these happy memories.

"By the way, I want to see what is in my envelope," said the minister, fishing out his gift. It was three salmon flies—"lures" they call them, and the beauty of them was so great Grizel declared that *no* salmon could resist them!

"Donal Cattanach has been telling me that though one leaves Glen Craigan one must always come back. So you see, the swans are back, the fisher (not to call him a poacher) is back, Sir Duncan will come back, and bring his lovely dog. . . ."

He looked at her with laughter but fullest comprehension; he was still young, still in love with his wife, still in sympathy with all young folks.

"By the way," Mr. Mackay went on, "that tinker Jamie Stewart told me that many, many years ago there was a little church there—probably a popish building of some kind—when the Corrie was populated, and they called it 'the Kirk o' the Corrie'. My wife thinks *she* coined the name. I must tell her," he chuckled.

"Tell her she re-discovered it," Grizel laughed, "and that was quite equal to coining it."

Daylight lingers long in our northern land. In Corrie Street angry mothers were chasing rebellious bairns home to supper and bed. "It's no' time," they protested. "Look see, it's daylight yet."

From the open window of No. 7 came the sound of a wireless and a wistful negro song:

> "Ring-ro—the banjo,
>   I love that dear old song,
> Come list to me, my true love,
>   Where have you been so long?"

The dark of a summer's day always cast a pensive feeling over Grizel, and to-night the question in the song made her sigh wistfully.

"How long is it before your husband returns?" Mr.

Mackay asked in a polite chatty way. Their eyes met and both laughed.

"One year, ten months," she sighed.

"You didn't mention *days* or *hours*," he said quizzically. . . .

In the manse garden Kit straightened her back and regarded her handiwork with much complacency. A flower bed, that was what she was trying to fashion, when the car with the doctor and the minister stopped at the gate.

And after exchanging greetings, Kit said, "Now, Tom, look at that patch of ground—what do you think it looks like?"

Tom frowned portentously and was silent. Then he spoke: "What do I think it looks like? It looks as if a benevolent pig had been rooting in it!"

"Oh—oh, Tom Mackay—you—you!" Kit spluttered with rage. "Suppose," she challenged, "*you* take the rake and the hoe and let me see what a benevolent *minister* can do."

"Kit, I would remind you I have on my Sunday breeks and coat—I even have my lum hat—you wouldn't like to see me gardening in all my present splendour?"

Kit led the way into the study, where a supper table was laid. "I'll just put a match to the cooker," she said. "Yes," turning to Grizel, "some angel has presented me with a Calor gas outfit—come on to the kitchen and see it. It makes me so happy I could dance with delight. No, I don't know in the least who sent it—I wish I did, so that I could let the kind donor know how I'm just *bursting* with gratitude.

"Do you remember Beth, in *Good Wives* I think it was, and how the child loved cooking things? I'm like that!

Look—an egg and cheese dish of a succulence not easily described! Here, you carry in the plates and I'll follow. Tea you shall all have and toast made on my grill." She pirouetted on her toes.

"Take care, woman," Grizel warned her, "there's not enough room in this kitchen for two able-bodied women, a Calor gas stove, *and* a boiling kettle—and a dancing dervish!"

"I have a few, a very few, strawberries," Kit whispered. "Hush, now, not a word till the minister says grace."

Johnnie Brandon and his young wife Sheila dropped in at this point. Johnnie had a parcel which he carried as tenderly as if it were a baby. "Out of our own garden," he boasted, and opened the parcel.

"Rhubarb! Pink!"

Tom looked wickedly at his wife. "Tell them," he urged, "how much you like rhubarb."

Kit's face was crimson. "Thank you very very much, Mr. Brandon, and take no notice of my husband's remarks. Long, long ago when I was a child, I had to take cod liver oil. Yes, it is truly awful stuff, and my mother always promised me if I took a spoonful *she* would give me a spoonful of jam—*rhubarb jam*. So you see rhubarb has somewhat unpleasant memories for me."

Everyone was laughing and capping Kit's story with one of their own. It was a thoroughly merry meal—how could it be otherwise when all around the table were friends, and shared jokes as well as meals?

"Sir Herbert and Johnnie and brother Reginald have all been surveying suitable sites for the new Recreation Hall," Sheila said when there was a pause in the general conversation.

gent remarks she was about to make on a tactful husband and a hateful new blouse. The moment she saw her guests, however, her anger died, and she knew that here were people she was going to like, friendly and kindly. Kit always remembers that her first (official) visitors were John Stewart and his wife, with their endearing smiles and warm handclasps.

John Stewart was a middle-aged man with a mop of iron-grey hair which stood bolt upright on his head, and he had a pair of friendly grey eyes which looked you straight in the face. His wife was a little woman with a worn, thin face and a pair of beautiful brown eyes. When her face was at rest there was rather a bitter look about her lips. She had, too, that excellent thing in women, a low sweet voice, though it did not necessarily follow that the words she uttered were either low or sweet, and the twinkle in her eyes was decidedly mischievous.

Tom, meantime, was proudly exhibiting the improvements they had made in the garden, carefully forgetting to mention how much had been done by Kit, and how much by himself.

"Let's sit out and enjoy the sunshine," he said, and carried out chairs for his guests. Kit curled herself up on a doormat, and Tom balanced himself on the garden fence. All prepared to talk and enjoy themselves.

"What a lovely place you have here, Mackay, and what a glorious view. The loch looks as blue as the sky."

"Yes," cried Kit in delight, "I've often rejoiced at the way the sky and the loch seem to say, 'How d'ye do' to each other. Don't you think the hills look lovely? In those dreary and cold days of February and March when we'd just come here, I used to think the hills looked unkind, austere and aloof. But not now . . . no, they are friends of ours, ready to protect us—I love them," she added with a warm note in her voice. "And presently they'll be wearing their royal purple robes of heather. I wish someone would invent an implement to root up the bracken, though; it keeps encroaching on good ground, and is of no use to anybody."

"Bulldozers," Mr. Stewart suggested. "My son Willie, when he was a little chap, used to stand fascinated watching the bulldozer yanking up the roots of trees in the new housing area. He thought it awfully cruel, though!"

"So it is," Kit cried. "Only God can make a tree! How old is your son Willie?—I didn't know you had a son."

"We have a son and a daughter," Mrs. Stewart said. "Our boy is at the Varsity, and our daughter is at Atholl Crescent." She looked earnestly at Kit as she spoke. "Do you know, my dear, you're at the happiest time of your life just now; your husband and your children beside you. ' 'Tis a woman's heaven to have all she loves beneath one roof'," she sighed.

"But don't they come home?" Kit asked.

"Yes, but not the way they left; they've new experiences, new views of their own, and you no longer share their interests. You don't know their new friends, and you wonder just what influence those friends are having on your children. Young people to-day are all bent on leading their own lives."

Kit remembered her mother saying very much the same, and she was thankful that as yet she had not had to part with her bairns.

"God says, 'Bring up this child for me,' and parents don't agree, they want to bring up the child for themselves, and when the child wants to bring himself up they're dismayed and hurt. No woman ever relished the idea that her cherished son is one day to give his heart to someone she doesn't know about and whom she already dislikes." She laughed, but there was pain beneath the laughter as she added, "Willie already speaks of his girl friends, and Alison has innumerable boy friends." She shook herself mentally and physically and went on: "We must keep remembering that we once upon a time took away some other woman's cherished son, and I'm afraid we did not always remember to be grateful . . . I wonder what our menfolk are discussing as they pace up and down the garden path?"

"They're examining our kail yard, I think, and discussing matters of ecclesiastical and economic interest—such as the Church extension business. It is one of the problems which are exercising all ministers at this time."

"Tell me, my dear, how you're getting on with life here—it must be a great change from your old home at St. James's?"

"It is," Kit agreed, "but I love it, and I love the manse, and the folks are very kind. Of course, we've a very mixed lot of people—all the factory workers are of different nationalities and different denominations, and you'd be surprised to find that the newcomers look down on the natives as 'Hielanders', while the natives look down on them as strangers. Yes, Tom has to walk warily in this place."

"He's the right man to do it," Mrs. Stewart said so warmly that Kit found her affection for her new friend growing apace. "You're lucky too," she went on, "to have come before the winter meetings begin. That gives you time to think and plan, for the kirk will pull you one way and the manse the other, especially if you've bairns in the manse."

"That is certainly going to be one of my problems," Kit admitted, "my children are so young."

"Look after them *first*," counselled her new friend. "Remember what the shepherd said when someone asked him how he had such good sheep? 'Because I care for the *lambs*,' he answered. Now I'm dying to see the inside of your manse. I've seen your garden, and I think it's wonderful."

"Take care of that step, then. This house was once a shooting lodge and it's full of surprises. It has a gun-room and a larder, and even a billiard room. We don't use any of them, of course."

"But what like is the kitchen range? More lives are ruined and homes made unhappy through a bad kitchen range than through lack of love."

Kit agreed, though she also suggested that love might play a part in their home life, too.

"You like living in a manse, don't you?" Mrs. Stewart went on. "I've been in three or four since I first married, and I still like it. The folks who come are delightful—ministers, I mean, though there are some exceptions, and the manse folks are expected to keep a sort of hotel. One gets a faddy visitor occasionally—wandering lecturers and such like—but give me the ministers every time who will sup their porridge and milk for breakfast and don't bother whether the fish is fried or steamed. You haven't met the Superior Sam yet, have you? He's a lecturer . . . with a tummy. . . ." She eyed Kit mischievously, who said, "You wouldn't want him without a tummy, would you?"

"No—but he dines late. 'I make it a rule never to eat

between lunch and dinner,' he'd tell you, scorning your afternoon tea, because it isn't China, and your bread because it isn't toasted and brown."

"I'll try to avoid the Superior Sam," Kit promised her, "or if he does come here I'll give him fish and chips, and I'll call our mid-day meal our dinner."

"My dear, he'd die on the spot. . . . Stay me with crumpets and comfort me with tea," Mrs. Stewart went on, when the two manse ladies had finished their tour of inspection and had finally arrived at the study. "How nice you've made this room look," she said, glancing at the many little personal touches which gave the room a homely look.

"I'll show you a device I have for keeping my husband's many papers and book catalogues tidy. Does your husband collect book catalogues? Mine does, and if I dare to light the fire with one it's sure to be the one he is looking for."

Both men entering the study at this moment uttered loud and bitter denials of hoarding book catalogues, until Kit ordered them both to come into the dining-room where she'd laid a "right" tea, Tom denouncing the afternoon variety.

Over the tea table, the talk was strictly churchy. The problem in Glen Craigan was the mixed nationalities of the people, how to reach them, how to unite Highlanders and strangers.

Mr. Stewart said, in his grave, considering voice, "Seek ye first the kingdom of God. Get to know your people, especially the children, and try to remember their names. If there are boys in the family, you can get the mothers, and the mothers will get the fathers. We have examples of that from the classics. Above all, don't judge hastily, as

I once did. A widow who was a dressmaker in my congregation kept me at arm's length for quite a while, and one day when I called on her I found her trying to thread a needle. 'Let me do that for you,' I said, and she burst into tears and confessed that her eyes were failing her, and she'd been afraid anyone would know. Aye, to know all is to excuse all."

Before Mr. Stewart could say more, there was the unmistakable sound of a car stopping at the garden gate.

"It's the Rev. Malcolm Maitland and his braw new wife," Mr. Stewart whispered, peeping out at the window. "Yes, yes, that's the exquisite Envira who owns and drives her own car. Malcolm, wise man, married money."

A short tubby little man was helping his wife to descend, though judging by the vigorous way she handled the car she needed no help. Then, throwing open the garden gate with the air of a courtier, the Rev. Malcolm Maitland showed his wife in, he himself following and carrying her coat and scarf.

By this time the party round the tea table had with one consent made for the door to welcome the strangers, Mr. Stewart doing the honours by introducing them all. The exquisite Envira looked, from the top of the absurdity of flowers and ribbon which she called a hat, down to her high-heeled shoes, as if she had stepped out of *Vogue*. Mrs. Stewart, like the brick she was, hastily gathered together the dirty tea dishes, brought in clean ones, and straightened the tea table, for which Kit blessed her. Meantime, John Stewart, looking at the clock, announced that if they were to catch the four-fifteen bus they would need to hurry. With many expressions of goodwill and promises to come back soon, they left Kit and Tom to deal with their next visitors.

"Yes, I'll remember," said John Stewart, in parting, "I'll come to your Communion in August."

Envira, like a ship in full sail, took possession of Tom's high chair, where she sat prepared to be admired. Her husband's expression as he gazed at her was one of maudlin adoration. And Kit noted with annoyance that Tom was also gazing admiringly at the lady from *Vogue*. Meantime, she dealt with the kettle in the kitchen, and oh! wicked Kit, she took her time about it too; then she hurried upstairs to powder her nose and made one more gigantic effort to get these maddening buttons to co-operate.

The exquisite Envira, having exhibited her immaculate stockings, her silken skirt, and her nylon blouse, opened her handbag and took out her cigarette case. She was smoking when Kit came to summon them to tea, and the dainty way she held and manipulated her cigarette in its holder told of long practice.

She turned to Kit and with a bright smile said, "You've quite a nice little manse here."

"It's not little," Kit flashed. (Oh, Kit!) "What like is your manse?"

Envira blew a smoke ring and answered, speaking with great deliberation, "Of course, it is much bigger than this—it was built in the days when maids were procurable. I managed to get two. Have you?"

"No," Kit said reluctantly, "I haven't even a daily."

Envira asked languidly what Kit was doing about her winter meetings; and what did Kit do with the rooms she did not occupy?

"I use the old billiard room for drying clothes in the wet weather. Now, please do come and have tea."

The Rev. Malcolm eyed the tea table with warm appreciation. It did not matter that his host and hostess had already had their tea—he wasn't the man to stand on ceremony. Also, Envira's idea of afternoon tea might be dainty, but how very insufficient.

It gave Kit much satisfaction to see how the two people did justice to their meal. "These are quite nice little sandwiches," Envira said, biting into her fourth. "The hill air here has made me quite hungry, and has made me forget that I'm slimming."

"I'm not," said her liege lord, spreading his scone with butter and jam.

The time came at last for them to depart, and Envira rose to make her farewells. "Well, I'm always at home every second Thursday between three and five, and just let me know when you are coming. Are you on the phone? No? You haven't a car? No? Well, come by bus!"

The Mackays looked after their guests with obvious relief. "Tom," Kit said, "why didn't you marry a woman with money, then you might own a motor car!"

"It was stupid of me," Tom admitted in meek tones.

"And if you did," Kit said (the inconsistent creature), "what a lot of fun you'd have missed. You might have had a wife who called you 'hubby'."

Chapter 13

A HIGHLAND COMMUNION

TO the Rev. Tom Mackay, brought up in all the ways of the Highlands, a Communion was to him a matter of custom; to Kit it was a wholly new experience.

In St. James's Church, at such a time, there might be a preparatory service on Saturday, and on Sunday some other city minister might "exchange pulpits" with their own minister and on Monday there was—sometimes—a thanksgiving service.

In Glen Craigan, the first service began on Thursday, which was the Fast Day, and the last was the evening meeting on Monday.

It was, for the manse folk, a time of endless church services, of endless meals, when in August Kit had her first experience of what the Highlands called "*the time of the Sacraments*".

The congregation knowing that the manse "showed hospitality without grudging" sent, from the kindness of their hearts, all sorts of supplies of food, and Mrs. Macnab from the Kennels, knowing Kit's difficulties, came to help her with the cooking and the serving of the many stray meals. The cookery book, *Tried Favourites*, opened of its own accord at Beefsteak Pie, Steamed Pudding, and other succulent dishes.

Other problems were the starching and ironing of the "fair white linen cloths" used at the Communion season— these, like the polishing of the Communion vessels, were other experiences of which Kit had no knowledge. However, by Wednesday evening everything was in apple-pie order and Kit could relax until next day.

There was a ring at the bell, and a strange minister appeared. Kit heard Mrs. Macnab say, "Yes, sir, the mistress is at home, but the minister is not." Next moment the door opened, and it seemed the first minister for the Highland Communion had arrived—and a day too soon!

He belonged to the old school of ministers, which believed in dressing always in a way befitting the dignity of the Church; that is, in black frock coat and tall hat. His wife, as Kit afterwards discovered was fully as dignified as her husband, and dressed in sober, stiff silk dresses and black velvet mantles with jet trimmings. It was either owing to the fact that she had a Roman nose or that she wore such dignified clothes that the whole parish regarded her with respectful awe. But to return to Mr. Gillies who all this time was standing bag in hand.

He held out his other hand to Kit and introduced himself, regarding her in some perplexity. He had never seen a minister's wife quite like this, and he wasn't sure if he approved. But by the time Kit had him settled at the study fire with his pipe going comfortably and the prospect of a meal in the immediate future, he began to reconsider things; and when Tom arrived he found them fast friends.

The first service began at eleven o'clock, and believe it or not it went on till three! Kit used to say in her unregenerate moments how anyone could keep their minds on spiritual matters for such a long time was more than she could understand!

With the best will in the world, visions of a spoiled

dinner would appear; burnt-out fires or a burnt-out manse were the pleasing thoughts she had as she sat demurely in the manse seat. Then she remembered with thankfulness that Mrs. Macnab was there, and she'd keep things going.

Mr. Gillies was a preacher of the old school, a Highland mystic with strange ways of putting things, and Kit, unused to this particular kind of doctrine, listened carefully.

Tom had asked one or two elders to join them at dinner. At that somewhat solemn meal, the talk was all about Church extension—how was it to be managed, and where was the money to come from? Both these problems had to be faced.

Tom himself was much too busy to give much thought to the problems that day. When he sped Mr. Gillies on his way, he also welcomed Mr. Gilchrist, who was to assist at the "men's day" on Friday. A strange service this Friday one, said to be a survival of the old days of Cromwell, when the people thirsted for pure doctrine. The Highlander is, by nature, of a brooding, meditative mind; the environment and circumstances in the midst of which his life is set draw forth this natural bias, and the "men" must brood and think and meditate.

There are some people whose very presence in a house is helpful. David Gilchrist can best be described by the adjective "friendly"—he was the embodiment of friendliness; his brown eyes, his sudden and delightful smile, his vigorous handshake—for which he apologized next moment—and his voice all had this characteristic. Wherever he went he made friends and he never lost one. Between him and the Glen Craigan manse folks there was a bond which only strengthened with the years.

One of the great joys and privileges of a Highland

manse is the talk by the study fire, when the day's work is done. Mr. Gilchrist came from Lewis, and had all the strange mysticism of that island whose inhabitants are the descendants of prophets, priests and kings. Queer tales he had to tell of his home. Second sight he believed in, as indeed did Tom Mackay, and Kit listened in astonishment as the men capped each other's tales.

Uistean Mhor and the *Breabadair Bhuie* (Yellow Weaver) was one of the tales Tom told, one of the weirdest of Celtic folk tales. It is really a variant of the were-wolf story, found in so many countries. Mr. Gilchrist's tales were of personal experiences. Going home one frosty evening, his way took him past a lonely churchyard. He noticed that the gate was open, and a newly-dug grave yawned eerily, close by the wall. Further along the road he met a phantom funeral. Shadowy figures were carrying the coffin. Just as he got alongside the coffin, the sergeant in charge of the bearers called, "Relief". Immediately the two men carrying the head of the coffin stepped out, the two at the foot stepped forward, and as David, cap in hand, watched the scene, the sergeant beckoned to him to take his place at the coffin foot, along with a shadowy figure. Like a man in the grip of an awful nightmare he obeyed; on the frosty road his were the only footsteps that rang out, the others moved silently; an unearthly chill seized him, the coffin felt as heavy as lead, but still he moved forward. Then the cry of "Relief" rang out again; he stepped to the head of the coffin, his ghostly companion doing the same, and on again moved the grim company. At the churchyard gate he heard once more the cry of "Relief"—and then he fell in a dead faint. How long he lay on the cold road he never knew, but when he came to himself the moon had set, and he stumbled home in the darkness. There was, for weeks after, a deep bruise on his shoulder where the coffin had pressed.

"I'm afraid to go to bed," Kit said, shivering and drawing nearer the fire. "Tell me more." It was then they discovered the lateness, or rather earliness, of the hour, and it was decreed that the other tales must keep till the next day.

The next speaker was Dr. Lindsay, whom we know better as 'The Doctor', a man to whom we need give no introduction. He looked at Kit with laughing eyes, and told her that when her husband got obstreperous he would "sort him", while he added with dancing eyes, "I'm sure he'll always be in the wrong, and you'll always be in the right."

He prayed that evening, and his prayer was something the manse folk never forgot. God was very near, as the old man pleaded that the "covering wings might be spread around, and that on the morrow, the great day of the Feast, they might have a sense of His presence, and the peace of God that passeth all understanding." One, at least, of the listeners felt the fret and worry of the past, and the nameless dread of the future, passing away, as the old saint prayed. It was a fitting heart preparation for the services of the morrow.

The autumn sunshine next day was golden and warm; it seemed as though summer were loath to go. The trees in their changing dress, a passion of gold and crimson, were motionless beneath the blue sky, and the very river seemed to doze gently between its bracken-covered banks. A robin's wistful note gave an air of pensiveness to the scene, perhaps the only hint that summer was really gone.

Early the folks began to gather from far and near, the

influence of the day already to be seen in their quiet expectant faces. The elders, clad in their decent "blacks", their spotless linen a credit to their womenfolk, took their places in the seat below the pulpit. The communion table, covered with its linen cloth, had upon it the sacred and solemn elements. The atmosphere of the church was a reverent one, for the Scottish Highlander is at his best and highest when he is exercised in religious matters. People took their places quietly; the tables at which the Supper was to be celebrated were left empty. When the sacrament was being dispensed, the communicants would take their places and "remember the Lord". Meanwhile a hushed expectancy was on every face, there was silence except for the cautious step of the worshippers as they slipped into their places; outside, the church bell had ceased its calling. . . .

Then the side door opened; the beadle showed in the tall, dignified figure of the old minister.

"It's——" whispered Elspeth Bruce, nudging her mother.

"H-hush——" she whispered back, but the eyes of both women glowed. They had been expecting great things, and they were to get them too.

The golden sunshine pouring in through the window lighted the face of Dr. Lindsay as he opened the old Bible. "Let us sing to the praise of the Lord, psalm twenty-three," he began. "The bairns' psalm, the psalm that will help us from the cradle to the coffin", and they sang it to the tune "Evan".

The old minister read the fifteenth chapter of Luke, the mere listening to which makes hearts tender, and when he took for his text, "My son was dead and is alive again," the folks leaned back in their pews; but their spirits were

it was no longer possible to abide on the mountain top, when Monday and the toil of the week were waiting at the mountain foot.

"Oh, thou my soul, bless God the Lord," they sang to the tune of "Coleshill", and they sang it with moved hearts.

At night the church was packed, and the preacher again had a great uplifting word for the folks. He knew that his hearers were poor people, men dwelling remote from the throng and bustle of the city, and he preached of "One who was rich yet for our sakes became poor."

The old man was tired and spent by the time he was finished. He preached 'as a dying man to dying men' and the price he paid for his earnestness was a big one. He lay back very white-faced in Tom's study chair and allowed Kit to fuss over him to her heart's content; what woman worth her salt doesn't love to be so exercised!

They parted next day reluctantly, and when the old minister asked them both to come and be his guests for a few days they accepted with joy. Among the treasures Kit has kept from that time is a letter written to her by the old man, when already the shadow of the valley was falling on his face (but not on his heart, for it was always in the light of God's sunshine). A joy and a privilege to meet such a man; would God there were more of them! Their memory and name are as a fragrant perfume.

By Monday, everyone was feeling somewhat jaded, especially the manse folks. "Three more sermons," Kit groaned. "I envy the heathen!"

"Hush, hush," Tom replied.

"I won't hush," Kit said crossly. "If you had to be continually turning out bedrooms, and changing sheets and towels, you would say, 'Me for the Fiji Isles and the palm leaf!' "

Monday's man was Mr. Craig, a young and careless youth, who arrived carrying what looked like a jar of marmalade. This he deposited on the study mantelpiece remarking, "I hope you can lend me shaving tackle and pyjamas. I haven't brought any, but I've brought my own 'baccy. The stuff you smoke, Mackay, I remember of old."

"How long do you expect me to preach?" he next demanded. "Remember, I'm to read my sermons!" He had eyes light and full of dancing madness, which made Kit think of Alan Breck; indeed it was by that name he got to be known ever after. An understanding, warm-hearted, loyal young fellow who reduced his hearers to helpless laughter by his mimicking of "the good and godly old wives", but a man who would trudge miles through the snow to read to a sick ploughman. His sermons, however, were quite orthodox.

As each man departed, an envelope with his expenses was handed to him, a ceremony which struck Kit as very strange, but which Tom and his helpers took in the most matter-of-fact fashion. Mr. Craig even complimented him on his promptness and said, "That ruffian in Loch Onie has never given me my expenses since his last communion. Watch yon man, Mackay. He'll invite you to social meetings, and communions and thanksgivings, and give you his blessing on departure; a fat lot of good that's likely to do, when you don't know where you're to get your next ounce of tobacco."

Chapter 14

A PUBLIC MEETING

A Public Meeting to discuss the Building of a new Recreation Hall in Glen Craigan will be held in the hall on Friday 17th at 7.30 p.m. All interested in this scheme are invited to be present.

COPIES of this notice, printed in fat black letters, were distributed from Corrie Feor to the Chanonry and aroused much interest. Rumours regarding such a hall had been in the air for some time, the source possibly being Captain Reginald Mortimer-Jones, brother of the industrious Mrs. Paterson. To take immediate and decisive steps was *not* the way of the folk of Glen Craigan; they had to talk over it, discuss it, and then—then— they'd see!

"Who'll be at the bottom of this?" Donal Cattanach wondered. "There's yon craitur Grant, Cyril Grant, him that used to work in Inverness and used to part his hair in the middle and wear a gold ring on his pinkie—d'ye think he's anything to do wi' it?"

Peter-postie, who, in his official capacity as postman, knew all about the Glen folks' letters, said very decidedly, "It's more like Captain Reginald Mortimer-Jones— Mrs. Paterson's brother."

"Oh, the army man," said Cherlie-the carrier, and everyone laughed, and Donal said, "I don't believe it."

"Weel, weel, time will tell," quoth Peter who did not

129   I

handle letters without a shrewd suspicion as to the different writers and receivers.

"It's far mair likely the *Boddach-na'-muc* is at the bottom o' this. Since his bairn was born he's forever speaking aboot child welfare work, an' telling mothers o' families how to bring up their bairns—he's an auld wife, an' never in all my life did I see a man so foolish aboot a bairn: you'd really think no man ever had one but himsel'," said Cherlie.

"Weel, it's the first one ever he had. He's wanting a place for a baby clinic, whatever that means—such nonsense! And for a place where the young folks can play games. What's wrong wi' a game o' shinty, an' ye dinna need a hall for fitba'."

Donal Cattanach immediately took up the other side. "Playacting—couldn't Glen Craigan take that up, same as they did in Dingwall?" He was all in favour of giving the young folks a dancing hall, and it was supposed the lady doctor thought that too.

So public opinion swayed this way and that—the first and perhaps the most vital question being, "Who's to pay?"

The village hall was filled to capacity the night of the meeting, and gave one reason for a bigger hall being needed. The present one was much too small and most inconvenient. A crowd bigger than the crowd inside queued outside the door, trying to squeeze in. Peter-postie was firm with them, and with all gate-crashers— why even Rory-the-post from Muirton with his "Stand back there" was treated with contempt.

Jim-the-vanman with Sheila Thompson, the new merchant's daughter, charged in, saying as he did so, "Haud back yourself, pot-belly," and in they surged.

In such a packed audience it was not easy to make oneself heard. All the same, Captain Reginald Mortimer-Jones managed it, first by rapping on the floor with a heavy stick and then by using his voice, and he, being an army man, could do that most effectively.

"I propose we ask Sir Herbert Higgins to take the chair," he shouted.

"I second the motion." By craning their necks and straining their eyes the Glen folk could just see that the seconder was Mr. Cyril Grant, looking more like a barber's clerk than ever.

Sir Herbert was duly dug out of the seat in front—it needed a united effort to do this, so tightly were they packed. He mounted the little platform, which truth to tell did not look any too steady.

Sir Herbert, wearing his hairiest plusfour suit, his most intimidating-looking brown brogues and holding the sort of stick Harry Lauder used to carry, bowed and smiled and evidently spoke though no one could catch a single word. That was because of the storm of applause which greeted him.

Donal Cattanach, sitting beside Sandy Morrison the merchant, nudged him and whispered in his ear, "See you to the mannie! Wasn't myself frightened he'd be wearing his kilt? The last time I saw him in it it was so long at the back it was doon to the calves o' his legs, an' so short in front it showed his knee-bones."

"That's because his pot-belly took it up in front," Sandy explained kindly.

"Oh, whatever you say yourself, Sandy," Donal agreed amiably, then he added, "When we come oot o' this meeting I'll mebbe have a little message for you." There was awful significance in his voice. Sandy understood, and nodded, and said, "Very well, just man."

The storm of cheering now died down, and Sir Herbert feeling, if not exactly looking, like a feudal laird, spoke well and forcibly. There was no doubt he knew how to handle a crowd, to arouse their interest and to keep them interested.

A new hall? Well, couldn't they look around the present one crowded to suffocation, and did they need to ask the question? The Glen was growing and was likely to go on growing. He'd just had a meeting with his fellow directors, and they were anxious to build another factory, perhaps two; the demand for the famous Glen Craigan tweed was daily growing, and they were now ready to weave the wool-and-silk tartans, which were so popular in warmer countries. This was a most tactful beginning, and opened the door for the rest of his speech. "We must work 'ard," he said, "to meet these orders, but all work and no play makes Jack a dull boy." They wanted to make the workers happy, and only when you're happy can you do your best work. They would like to put up a good play, a cheery dance—yes, he was all for the country dancing class (in a confidential tone he told them why, as if they didn't know that his wife was a country-dance teacher!) By this time the audience was in high good humour and certainly in sympathy with Sir Herbert.

"We should like to hear any other speakers," Sir Herbert said, sitting down and wiping his brow. "It's 'ot," he confided to the minister, who was sitting beside him.

The silence which always follows such an invitation was broken at long last by Henry Sinclair, whose croft marched with that of William Macleod of the High Muir. Two men more unlike could not possibly exist, yet an odd friendship flourished between them.

Henry was a tall gaunt old man who somehow reminded one of an eagle, with his keen bright eyes, his straggling grey hair and his nose as sharp as a beak. He, like the new merchant, Sheila Thompson's father, belonged to a very select church in Polussie, and denounced the present day for all its frivolities and sinfulness. Yet beyond denouncing all these he did nothing to help to make the world a brighter place.

"Sir," he began, "you are talking about a new hall. A lot of nonsense." He thumped his stick angrily on the floor.

"Hear! Hear!" Donal Cattanach encouraged him. (Oh, Donal!)

"They are now learning the bairns to sing and act and dance." He paused for a moment and looked balefully around. "Better for them to learn the bairns to read their Bibles and say their carritches. Better for the ministers too to go round the houses and ask bairns and parents to say their questions. Do they do that?" he challenged. "*No, they do not!*"

"Thank goodness," whispered Mrs. MacGlashan. "I never could say 'Effectual Calling'."

"And they'll be wanting a stage," he went on—he spoke the word as if it were poisonous—"they'll destroy body and soul. And they're wanting cloakrooms, too, and rooms where babies can be examined . . ." He paused for a moment glaring angrily.

To everyone's surprise it was the Muirton District Nurse who answered him, a shrewd level-headed lass from Aberdeen. Her cheeks were red, her eyes were bright. "Sir Herbert, may I speak? This gentleman, whose name I do not know, possibly there are no young folks in his house, will be interested in the statistics of the last number of years. He can study for himself what child welfare work has done for mothers and babies. The number of women dying in childbirth in the beginning of this century and compared with that of to-day will speak for itself. Our work is not only to help at the birth, but to visit the child and mother afterwards—to give good advice and to see that it's taken, and so guard the child that there will be no further wastage of child life. This wastage has been in the past simply appalling, but with our present-day nursing associations and clinics much has been done, though there is still much to do, and I hope the day is not far distant when in this growing and prosperous Glen we shall have a good well-equipped clinic." With flashing eyes she turned to look at Henry Sinclair. She did not hear a cynical remark made by Mrs. MacGregor, the far-from-satisfactory foster-mother of Chrissie Robertson. "Set her up, indeed! Her to speak aboot bairns, an' her a no-merriet woman." It was clearly impossible for a "no-merriet" woman to know anything at all about child welfare!

Captain Reginald Mortimer-Jones, just to show that he knew a thing or two mounted the platform and bowing to Sir Herbert said, "Ladies and gentlemen, you will say that as I am a newcomer to the Highlands I have no right to speak. Perhaps I have not, but will you allow me to say a few words, because I love what I have seen of this beautiful land of yours, and because as a greatly-travelled man who has noted much during his life I can see the immense possibilities which the future holds for this Glen. Take welfare work, for instance." He proceeded to give them some "brute beasts" of facts, reading out of a long paper, the very sight of which scared the audience. The speech was received in antagonistic silence.

"Him an' his travels," snorted Peter-postie. "What did he travel for?"

"*Gas*, maist likely—it's what he has plenty o'."

Still he made out a good case for the hall, and were it not that he was a Sassenach, and were it not that the Glen folks were hopelessly prejudiced, he would have received a most sympathetic hearing.

Sandy Morrison now rose to his feet. He was a fine-looking old man, and there was something in his personality and in his bearing which impressed his hearers. What Sandy said *went*.

"Sir Herbert," he began, "ladies and gentlemen, I have lived in this Glen all my life, so you'll allow me to speak for the rest of the Glen people. I've seen with sorrow family after family leaving the place—death has been much among us, so has emigration. We've but to look at the ruins of empty houses which tell their own sad story. Yes, I know that just now things are prosperous— money is plentiful—the mills and factories are busy—Sir Herbert tells us good news of all that: *but*, my friends, how long will it last? This hall will cost thousands, and how is the money to be raised? We *may* get a government grant, which must be repaid, but to go on with this scheme is madness. It's to put a burden round our necks that will last all our lives, and will be a burden to the children who come after us. The Bible tells of the man who wanted to build a tower, but before he did so he sat down and counted the cost, to be quite sure he had enough money to finish it. My dear friends, don't you think we should do the same? Why, the very upkeep of such a hall, rates and taxes, lighting and heating, will cost a big sum. I move before we decide on this important matter we go home and think it over."

He sat down in gloomy silence, a silence which was shared by all his hearers.

"Good-bye to our recreation hall," whispered Jim-the-vanman to Sheila. "I suppose," he said dryly, "your father will be pleased."

Poor Sheila, she was already discovering the difficulty of a divided loyalty.

Sir Herbert looked down at the minister, who was sitting near the platform. "Have you anything to say, Mr. Mackay?"

Mr. Mackay rose. His friendly smile did much to dissipate the gloom. "Before saying anything definite," he began, in that intimate friendly voice of his, "will you please, Sir Herbert, and you, my friends, permit me to read you this cablegram which I have just received? I need not tell you that a certain lady whose husband is keenly interested in the doings of this Glen—for is it not his old home—has told him of this meeting. Here then, is a cablegram from our good friend, Sir Duncan Maclean." He held the envelope aloft. Excited cheering! "Listen, my friends, to what's in this cablegram:

"Good luck to you all—success and prosperity—best wishes for the new hall. Am forwarding first subscription of fifty pounds. More to follow, Duncan Maclean'."

The minister stood still, smiling happily at the faces which smiled happily back at him. Then he spoke. "After hearing such a message coming from the other side of the world to us to-night, and from such a friend, I have pleasure in moving that we go on with the new recreation hall."

Johnnie Brandon, armed with a note-book and fountain pen, was beckoned to the platform by Sir Herbert, who whispered something in his ear. This something made Johnnie shout, "Sir Herbert wants me to put down his name for another first subscription, with 'more to follow'. Who comes next?"

They *all* came next, and sums ranging from twenty pounds to half-a-crown were subscribed, and the new hall was no longer a dream, it was, after to-night, a reality. One must not forget to do justice to Captain Reginald Mortimer-Jones, who said, "My contribution is to get my nephew, a talented young architect from London, to draw up plans—one or two—for a recreation hall."

"We must have a committee," said Kit, glancing at her watch. "I wonder what's the right time? It's after elders' hours, I fear."

It took some time for the crowd to get out and one could overhear all sorts of opinions, but all agreed it was late.

"I wish," said someone, "we had a really reliable clock, either on the hall or on the church."

It was quite a stray remark, and no one, either speaker or hearers, guessed what would be the outcome of that speech.

Chapter 15

YOUNG SANDY

"THE drive is the most important shot in golf."

The speaker was Bill Balfour, the golf professional from Craigdhu, and the listener was Sir Herbert Higgins.

"Every man should 'ave an 'obby," he explained to his friends. Up to the time of his marriage, business had been his only hobby, but now with the coming into his life of the happy companionship of his wife and the marvellous possession of a son, Sir Herbert's sense of values had changed.

Around his dear ones all his plans now centred. Young Sandy, a fat, well-nourished, heedless child, sucked his thumb and played with Jinx, his puppy, blissfully ignorant of all the plans and schemes which his father had for him.

And his father wanted—oh, he wanted—with feverish intensity that his son should be proud of him, not only as a man of business, but as a man of many interests; hence, by some course of reasoning, came Sir Herbert's rather belated desire to play golf. He pictured himself and his son setting out, armed with clubs, for the golf course, and talking learnedly about clubs and balls, strokes and holes. It was a thrilling thought.

In the meantime, golf: and he meant to master it, for he had mastered more difficult things. Being as yet ignorant of the tantalizing game, one could only feel sorry for him.

"The swing," repeated Bill Balfour, and swung, oh, so swiftly and so effortlessly, his driver over his shoulder and sent the imaginary ball spinning out of sight.

"A short, thickset person finds more freedom standing away from the ball and must not lean forward"—thus the golf instructor. Then he added, "A short person like you would actually need a longer club."

It says much for Sir Herbert's anxiety to learn the "ancient and royal" game that he took these directions in good part. He made a sporting but laughably ineffective effort to swing.

"It's 'ot," he murmured, and shed his golf jacket.

"Do not jerk," went on the remorseless instructor. "Raise the left hand a little, brace back to the right, turn at the waist as far as possible——" That was unnecessarily cruel! How could one who had no waist "turn as far as possible"?

The long spell of rain had made the ground soggy, and the Lodge lawn, upon which they had been practising, was very much against the swing.

"Let's try the high road—there's a good stretch of grass, right from the bridge to the back of the manse."

Sir Herbert's wife, with young Sandy toddling rather shakily by her side, came out to watch teacher and pupil.

"I'd like to learn, too," said she.

"Not in these high-heeled shoes," warned her husband, speaking as though he were a well-seasoned golfer, "and you'd better get on some garments suitable for the game. We'll go on—yes, I'll take charge of young Sandy, and you hurry after. We'll take the high road, so's I can get decent ground for the swing."

He lifted his son on his shoulder, along with his split-new golf bag of clubs, and with Jinx capering gaily at his heels, and his pockets full of golf balls, he led the procession off.

The river path, high above the river itself, was in many ways an ideal spot for practising the swing—the only danger was that a ball might fall down and could not be retrieved.

"I'll have a whack," Sir Herbert said, and swung his burdens off his back. Young Sandy and Jinx immediately began a game of "tig".

"I feel," said Sir Herbert, "as if I could 'it the lighthouse across the bay," and he gazed rapturously at the ball. . . .

"Don't lift your head—keep your left arm straight—your right elbow down, and aim for the rough." In following these somewhat bewildering directions, Sir Herbert forgot his son . . . and next moment there was an agonizing cry as Sandy slipped and fell. Sir Herbert looked down the cruel, rocky riverside, and saw the angry waters of the Torran. The child, however, was lying on a little rocky shelf, so narrow that if he turned he would certainly fall into the river. His father stood frozen with horror. White-faced he stared at his companion. "My son—my son!" he cried. The anguish in his voice caused physical pain to his hearer.

The minister, coming home and taking a short cut through the moor, heard the cry and saw the awful reason for it.

"How in God's name are we to reach him?" asked the distracted father.

"Wait," cried Tom Mackay, and took a short, comprehensive look at the situation. He set off with lightning speed for the manse, which, fortunately was not very far

"Afraid it was me? No, no, I didn't learn rock-climbing in St. Kilda for a little loose stone to frighten me."

Bill Balfour was curiously examining the rope which had done such wonderful work. "I've never seen a rope like that. What is it made of?"

By this time they had gathered round the study fire, the minister looking like a brigand with a white bandage on his brow. Sir Herbert, his son sleeping soundly in his arms, sat on the other side of the hearth, and Donal Cattanach pretending to be "black-affronted" was quite pleased to sit beside Bill Balfour. All listened eagerly to the tale of the rope.

"When I was a student, the church sent me for a summer session to the island of St. Kilda. It's evacuated now, but then there were a few families living on it, and I was supposed to look after their spiritual welfare—it was quite a queer experience! The Islanders were quite unlike the other Hebridean folks, who are mostly crofters and fishers; the Kildean people are fowlers, rather than fishers, a people apart, with an ancestry and tradition you cannot find in any part of Scotland. They had sheep—not many, but the wool was beautifully silky. I think Seoras Gunn has a St. Kilda sheep, hasn't he, Donal?"

Donal knew, of course, and hadn't he helped Seoras to clip it, and wasn't the sheep called *Caora Bheag* (little sheep)?

"When a St. Kilda bride was married, the dowry she brought her husband was a bag of downs and feathers, and a *rope*. A queer dowry, wasn't it? Yes, it was for hanging—not the bridegroom, of course, but for hanging over the steep cliffs where the men gathered fulmars for oil and seabirds' eggs for eating. When the Glasgow steamers came in, in springtime, there was always a lot of eggs and wool to be sold. Long generations of rock-climbing had hardened the Islanders' muscles, especially their big toes, which were as useful to them as a thumb is to us. Bare-footed they scrambled down the face of Conagher, their feet holding them in safety while their hands gathered the eggs. Well, I was a young chap then, and more or less at a loose end—there wasn't enough to do; so I began to climb and tried to do the things the others did. Old Alastair Mackinnon gave me my first lesson, and rated me soundly for wearing shoes and so retarding the usefulness of the big toe. When I was leaving, Alastair gave me his blessing and this rope—it is made of heather roots, so light it can float in the water and so strong it will pull you up; well, you saw to-day what it held up." He finished with a smile, and it was at this point a very agitated young woman burst into the room—Sir Herbert's distracted wife, in fact.

"Is Sandy all right?" she gasped, and had a look to reassure herself, then she explained she had duly followed the golfers, but there was no trace of them, and something in the trampled grass made her uneasy, and so she had to hear once more the tale of the rope and the wonderful rescue of their first-born child. With a white face she shuddered as she listened, and had to try to take Sandy out of his father's keeping so as to be quite, *quite* sure he was all right.

"He wouldn't be sleeping so soundly if he were not," Kit assured her. "Now, will you all come and have tea? Daisy and Tommy have just come in from school—they'll love to see Sandy . . . I see he's awake now."

The guests who gathered round the tea-table were typical of the manse folk who literally "showed hospitality without grudging", and were themselves all the richer because of it.

"Say 'Grace'," the minister said, nodding to the children.

They folded their hands, shut their eyes and repeated a Grace so comprehensive that it needs nothing added to it:

> "Thank you for the world so sweet,
> Thank you for the food we eat
> Thank you for the birds that sing,
> Thank you, God, for everything."

Sir Herbert looked and listened; he also made a mental note that when his son was a little older he too would be taught that Grace.

Chapter 16

THE KIRK CLOCK

A SHARED experience such as Sir Herbert and the minister had had is not easily forgotten; its consequences are much more far-reaching than anyone can realize. Between the men a link had been forged which would abide as long as they lived.

Sir Herbert's heart went out in a deep sense of gratitude to the minister, and because of its very depth he could not give it utterance. The minister, with his brotherly kind heart, appreciated the other's inarticulate gratitude and responded.

Sir Herbert wished above all things to show his gratitude with a gift. He remembered with a pang of regret how he had once blundered, with his stupid feet, on to the feelings of Miss Harriet Brodie. "I'll tell one of my gillies to chuck a pair of bunnies over your garden wall," he had said; he recalled still the gentle but dignified snub his words had evoked from the lady. She and Dr. Grizel Gillespie had had quite a good hand in teaching him something about a sense of delicacy. He had learned his lesson; he was not to offer a gift to the minister, as if it were a reward for saving his son's life; it must be something impersonal and delicately offered.

He consulted Johnnie Brandon, his old friend and fellow-worker. When it is mentioned that when the two men were together they were always "Bert" and "Johnnie", we can understand their relationship.

Johnnie quite saw the problem and the difficulties. Nothing personal must be offered. "But," cried Johnnie, "what about something for the kirk? I notice every minister is delighted with a gift to his kirk. I've heard Sheila and her father discussing kirks and presentations."

As Sir Herbert knew nothing about kirks and presentations and ministers, he was willing to be guided by one who did.

"What could I give?" he asked helplessly.

"Well, there's a baptismal font—they haven't one now. A new reading desk? A carved communion table? Chairs?" Quite a bewildering selection, evidently.

Sir Herbert looked perplexed, and lighted a cigarette to help his thinking; so did Johnnie, and after a thoughtful pause during which Johnnie's cigarette burnt his fingers he cried, "I have it—a *clock*."

"What sort of clock?"

"A kirk clock—one that everyone in the Glen can see. Why," he said with a chuckle, "if we had a good clock I'd have hopes of making the Glen a punctual place, and that when we say seven o'clock we don't mean seven-thirty or eight! It would help our workers," he went on, "they are always at variances as to the correct time."

Bert (as we take the liberty of calling him) lit a second cigarette and took a second thought.

"I like the idea, Johnnie," he said, "but where could we put it?"

"Over the front door, of course."

"But then it would not be seen by everyone."

"No-no. . . . Tell you what, Bert—let's go and take a look at the kirk." Johnnie believed in striking the iron while it was hot. "Let's look where would be the best place. You want everyone to see it?"

"Well, Johnnie, that was *your* idea."

"So it was," Johnnie said airily. "Let's take a look at the building and think it over."

Soon they were examining the church. "We want the clock to be where everyone can see it," Johnnie repeated.

"I don't see how that can be done." Bert was seeing difficulties—Johnnie was not.

"It's a good thing the kirk stands high." Johnnie led the way to the front door. "We could put it above the door," he suggested. Already in his mind he had decided that a tower must be built for the clock, but like the diplomat he was he did not *say* so; there were various ways of suggesting it!

Bert, in blissful ignorance, gazed at the church door, and after a long pause he said: "A clock would not be much use stuck up there."

"The folks going into the church would see it."

"But we want the folks who don't go in to the church to see it," put in Sir Herbert, who was himself no church-goer.

They were still examining possible positions and Johnnie had offered to get specifications and plans, when Captain Reginald Mortimer-Jones, with Cyril Grant, passed along and paused to greet them. Thanks to the military man the Recreation Hall was making excellent progress, and all things being equal they hoped to open it in February. Sir Herbert, whose keyword was " 'ustle", had certainly done a lot to bring this about. He had bombarded friends near and far for subscriptions, and funds, that all-important matter, were now fairly satisfactory.

The Captain asked: "What are you doing about the church?"

"Nosey-parker," muttered Johnnie, but Sir Herbert, less knowing, told what they had been thinking about.

148

"A clock for the church? Where are you to place it?"

"We have not decided yet; possibly over the front door."

They all gazed critically at the door, and Cyril Grant volunteered the information that it would make the church look like a stable. Even when the others disagreed he stuck to his guns, which made Sir Herbert very angry, but it also made him more determined than ever that the clock should not be put over the church door. Johnnie seconded his resolution, and added daringly to the others, "Of course, Sir Herbert was to build a tower for the clock—it is to be his gift to the church, and"—he turned to Sir Herbert and said, "weren't you thinking of having a clock with four faces? Yes, that's your idea— that would be a real and valuable asset."

"I don't see that the church needs a clock," grumbled the Captain, not at all pleased at Johnnie's suggestions.

Sir Herbert was frankly amazed at the audacious suggestions made by Johnnie. A clock, yes, but certainly not a tower, and certainly not a four-faced clock. He gave Johnnie a look which said, "Wait, my man, till we're alone, and I'll have something to say to you."

But Johnnie was quite equal to him. When the others had taken their way again he said, "I wanted to take the wind out of their sails, and of course you needn't build a tower and a four-faced clock—I only said it to impress them. You can put the clock over the front door——"

"And make the kirk look like a stable?" Bert's voice was indignant. "No, Johnnie, I was rather taken aback when you spoke, but, dash it all, man, I'll not go back on you. I'll build a tower and get a clock worthy of the church and its minister."

"Hurrah," Johnnie applauded, "that'll sort that interfering military man."

As Captain Reginald and his henchman went home, they pondered over this new scheme.

"I don't see that the church needs any clock, but we do need a good clock on the Recreation Hall! It would look well, and be of great use. Suppose, now, we suggest to Sir Herbert that the right place for the clock is on the hall. . . ."

They discussed the matter thoroughly, and finally decided that they'd call on Sir Herbert (when Johnnie Brandon was out of the way!) and point out to him his error in judgment.

"You leave it to me, Grant," quoth the military man. "I'll make him see our point of view. You'll come with me, of course. You can state the views for the workers: I'll state it for the other folk."

They arranged a night suitable, after which full of lofty resolutions and admonishments they took their separate ways. The Captain discovered, to his annoyance, that his cigarette-case was empty: he must go after Grant and borrow a smoke and a match. And then both men went home, Cyril Grant pondering over the frequency with which the Captain borrowed his cigarettes.

tion Hall will be open all the time, and its uses will be greatly enhanced if there is a reliable clock placed on the front. The committee agreed that this would be ideal, and would enhance the appearance of the hall, which, I may say without boasting, has been my daily care and occupation all these months."

Cyril Grant now took up the tale. "Captain Mortimer-Jones is too modest to mention the amount of work he has put in in connection with the hall, but any suggestion he makes should be carefully considered."

Sir Herbert offered his guests more cigarettes, he poked the fire, he rang the bell for refreshments, he did everything he could to put off time.

Pat Watson, duly primed, now "said his piece". He cleared his throat and began, "As a native of Glen Craigan and as a worker in Manchester, I know that good work has been done in both places, Sir Herbert. More and more people are coming to the Glen: I"—he gave a self-conscious little laugh—"I'm hoping to settle down here myself and to set up business one of these days; so perhaps I've a personal interest in urging that the clock should go on the Recreation Hall."

Sir Herbert smiled blandly—then he turned to Captain Reginald, his manner exceedingly polite. "Let us discuss the matter a little," he invited. "Your reasons are *all* good—I agree with you up to a certain point. You say the clock would be more useful on the hall than on the church. Would it be better seen?"

"Yes, if we built a tower for it," said the Captain.

"Oh, I see—I didn't realize you had planned to build a tower." Sir Herbert's tones were thoughtful. "Well, I shall be quite willing to give you the clock, seeing you are willing to build the tower."

"But—but——" stammered Cyril Grant, "we understood you were to give the clock *and* the tower."

"Oh, dear me, *no*!" cried Sir Herbert, "such a thought never entered my head. No, no, a *clock* I'm very willing to give you, but—that is all."

A stunned silence fell on them. The Captain's face flushed angrily, and his eyes, which were much too close together, had an evil gleam in them.

"When you and Mr. Brandon were discussing this matter the other evening, when we all met and had a chat, you certainly gave us to understand that *you* were to build the tower——"

"And make the clock a four-faced one." This from Cyril Grant.

Sir Herbert favoured him with a cool stare. "I'm afraid you did not understand. Mr. Brandon and I were discussing putting a clock on to the church; we decided where its place would be and that the clock should be four-faced. I cannot understand how you got the idea that I was to do this for the hall. I grant you that the addition of a tower and a clock on the hall would enhance its beauty. I suppose your committee could get an estimate for the building: oh, it may not amount to very much—five or six hundred pounds. You can budget for that, can't you?"

The atmosphere of the room became arctic; the deputation exchanged dismayed glances. Here was a state of matters for which they were not prepared, and which made them look absolute fools.

Before they could collect their scattered wits, Sir Herbert went on: "Of course the upkeep of the clock will need a little fund for itself. It will need repairing now and then, oiling, winding, cleaning and so on. You will,

I am sure, sink another hundred pounds for this purpose. The interest would be sufficient in ordinary circumstances—in fact," with a generous smile on his face he said, "when you have the clock duly installed in its tower, I'm quite willing to be responsible for its upkeep."

Never did a cat teasing a mouse enjoy itself more, though no one could guess this from Sir Herbert's inscrutable face.

The Captain sprang to his feet. "Sir Herbert," he snapped, "you are under a misapprehension." His voice was hoarse with suppressed fury. "The committee is not going to put a clock on the hall, nor build a tower for it either. I should like to say that in the cause of peace it would be well to let the matter drop. The workers were enthusiastic about the clock——"

"For which I was to pay." Sir Herbert's voice was gentle, but his face was not. "If, as you say, Captain, the people of this Glen have their affections set on a clock on the hall, then by all means let them buy one. My proposal was, and is, a clock for the church. Yes, I know, my first idea was merely a clock, and to put it as a mark of my gratitude to the minister of the church for saving my child—and me—from tragedy. Mr. Brandon and I went over the building—you remember, we met you?—and Mr. Grant said to put the clock over the church door would make it look like a stable. I must say it was these words of his that put the idea into my head that we should build a tower."

No one could be more polite, and when Betty and a tray came in he gave his wife a look which was surprisingly like a wink, as she pressed cups of tea and slices of cake upon her guests.

As they rose to depart, Sir Herbert repeated his

generous offer, and begged the deputation to report it to the committee. Out of kindness to these three disgruntled men, it is only right to suppress their remarks, as they went homeward, on the subject of the kirk clock.

The building of the church tower and clock marked another important milestone in the history of the Glen, and recalled to at least one or two people rather varied feelings on its origin.

The minister was wrestling with the highly controversial Epistle to the Hebrews in readiness for the November Communion—it was now late October and the days were getting shorter and shorter.

Sir Herbert was looking like a man who had a happy secret which he wishes to share with another. He came into the manse study with a folder of papers which looked like an architect's blue-prints.

"Take a look at these things," he said, sitting down, but keeping his eyes fixed on his friend's face to read by his expression what were his thoughts.

And the minister thought a great many things—all different—and not one near the reality. He looked in perplexity at the folder. "What does this mean, Sir Herbert?" he asked, a puzzled frown on his brow. But no frown could chase away the kind look in Tom Mackay's eyes.

"What do you think this is?" asked Sir Herbert, pointing to the papers.

"This—this blueprint looks like my kirk, only it's got a tower and a clock. Whiles I have wished it had."

He studied the papers again, then he gave a little sigh. Was it a longing one, or was it because he was very weary of the Epistle to the Hebrews?

Sir Herbert laughed rather constrainedly, and then said, "But do you like the look of it, Tom?" He uttered the name shyly—was he taking a liberty?

"I wish you'd call me Tom," said the minister, and went on, "Do please explain this. It certainly makes a wonderful picture of what my kirk would look like if it had a clock and a tower."

"It's what your kirk *will* look like when it gets a clock and a tower. Well, you know what I feel about last September—how you saved my boy's life. If he had been lost, I would have died——"

"Nonsense—don't get morbid. Anyway he wasn't lost, and you're not to die for a long time yet—not till you can play a decent game of golf and I can beat you at it." He fell to studying the papers again; you could trust Tom Mackay to bridge over any emotional moment in the happiest and most natural way.

Sir Herbert blew his nose rather loudly, and then he said, "Betty and I want to mark our gratitude to you, and we thought that a gift to the kirk would be——" His vocabulary wasn't equal to the situation.

"It's the very nicest thing you could do," Tom cried. "How did you think of such a thing? A clock—and a tower—I must tell Kit!"

Kit and her family were having a spirited argument on the subject of turnip lanterns. The scooped-out contents of a neep, she said, were not to be eaten, and if they ate such horrid things there would be nothing for it but castor oil.

Tom, followed by Sir Herbert, had entered the kitchen, and to their eternal shame be it noted they both sided with the children. Tom even recalled the days of his youth when the centre of a swede was far far nicer than a stupid woolly banana.

"Go out of here, both of you," Kit stormed. "I thought you'd uphold my authority. What do you want, Tom? Oh, all right, I'll come. Now, Daisy and Tom, don't eat another mouthful of raw turnip."

"Daddy did," piped up Daisy, fixing reproachful blue eyes on her mother's face.

That lady's feathers were distinctly ruffled when she entered the study. "You are no better than a couple of mischievous schoolboys," she stormed.

"Quite true, goodwife! Just take a look at these papers."

The storm passed quickly from her face—Kit's rage never lasted long. "What are these?" she asked. "I never could understand blueprints. Do tell me?"

Sir Herbert told her. She gasped in astonishment. She couldn't take it in, and said, "Please, Sir Herbert, say it all over again. I want to understand," and she tried to imagine what like the Kirk of the Corrie would look with that wonderful clock tower.

"It will be rather like St. Barnett's in Edinburgh," Tom said.

"It will be far far nicer than St. Barnett's," she flashed. "Oh, won't it be beautiful! Oh, Sir Herbert, I do think you're doing a lovely, lovely thing. When——?"

"Oh, now that you approve—right away. You know my pet word is *'ustle.* Yes, I know you all laugh at me for using the word."

Then both he and Kit noticed a change in the minister's face.

"What's wrong, Tom?" she asked.

"Before accepting this most generous gift to the Kirk of the Corrie," Tom said slowly, "I must consult my Kirk Session and Deacons' Court."

"For the lord's sake—whatever are these?" asked Sir Herbert. "Do explain."

Tom explained that as the church was the property of the Presbytery no alteration could be done to it without the consent of the Kirk Session composed of elders and deacons.

"But surely they won't object——?" Sir Herbert's voice sounded flat.

"Many men, many minds," Tom said, plainly hedging.

"But why should they object?" Sir Herbert persisted.

Tom could not tell him that the Session might object to receiving a gift to the Church from a man who was not a member, who seldom entered it.

"I'll call a meeting on Sunday," he said, "and lay the matter before them. Personally, Sir Herbert, I need not tell you how I feel about this gift." His hearty hand-clasp said much more than his words. All the same, he was sensitively aware that he had hurt his friend.

Sir Herbert was feeling a little nonplussed. He sighed as he tried to tell Betty all about it, in talking over the matter when he got home. "Truly you Scotch are an unpredictable people," he said.

"Especially if you call us *Scotch* instead of *Scots*," she said, and kissed him.

Young Sandy, staggering in on his fat legs followed by Jinx, put an end to the conversation. The child's hands stroked away any little sense of pain of which his father had been conscious. Why, young Sandy was also unpredictable. All the same, well—he liked him fine! And perhaps in time he would begin to understand his wife's country-folk.

It is good to be able to record that when the matter was laid before the Kirk Session they one and all heartily approved and sent their grateful thanks to Sir Herbert. So perhaps, after all, the Scots are not unpredictable!

Chapter 18

TWO LETTERS

FROM Dr. Grizel Gillespie to her husband (Sir Duncan Maclean):

> The But-and-Ben,
> Glen Craigan,
> New Year's Day.

My dearest dear,

Your welcome and oft-read cablegram has just come and I am writing an air-mail letter to say to you a Happy New Year. Do you realize, Duncan, that we can now say, "Next year we'll meet". True, this is only January, but the fact remains that next year you will be home, and this New Year having come *doesn't count*.

It's queer to think that you are sweltering under sunny skies while we here have been having the most terrific snowstorm even the oldest inhabitant can remember! These oldest inhabitants, I find, are very fond of saying they never remember such a rainy summer or such a bad harvest or such a severe winter. Pooh! always such unprecedented events!

All the same, we really did have a long, long time of snow, frost and burst pipes. The snow shut us up in the Glen, and for a few days we were in isolation; it was rather a nice feeling, silent, shut off from everything— only "the bens and the glens and the seven mountain moors" for company. All the same, we were very glad when Peter-postie arrived on a sledge. The children thought it was really Santa Claus, but this figure, bundled up in great coat and innumerable scarves, a balaclava helmet on his head, could not be Santa. And Peter-postie's face was certainly not in the least like the children's picture of rosy, kindly Santa. If I did not know Peter so well, I would have been intimidated at his scowling face with icicles on his eyebrows and moustache, and a drip at his nose. I asked for news—he spluttered, "It's thon— thon wife at the Sheiling: her and her menfolk have all gone away and left a little shivering half-starved lassackie in the house. She's neither food nor fire, by golly!"

He glared at me, and remembering how you, my dear, drew my attention to Chrissie Robertson left to the tender mercies of Tibby MacGregor at Tore Brae, I got into touch with the manse folks. Blessings on Tom Mackay's long legs and warm heart, Annie Ross (that's her name) is now in the manse, and judging by Kit's delight at having her for a helper she's likely to stay there. Tom will deal with her foster-parents and make the necessary arrangements. If Annie turns out as well as Chrissie, everyone, except Mrs. Paterson of the Sheiling, will be pleased.

More news? You'll be sorry to hear that Sandy-the-merchant is to retire. He says he is too old to deal with all the new problems. Jim-the-vanman who is a sort of forty-second cousin of his is to take over the business, and what's more he's now engaged to Sheila Thompson, whose father is the merchant at the other end of the village. Jim (I always knew he had brains if he'd only use them) has gone into partnership with his prospective father-in-law. It's a masterly stroke.

Donal Cattanach, the rascal, is all anxiety to start a class in bagpipe music whenever the Recreation Hall is finished, which I understand will be quite soon. All the people who live near the hall are signing a petition to stop Donal from starting such a class, so the *Boddach-na'-muc* will exert his authority.

Speaking of the hall reminds me of a sappy bit of news, not gossip, but coming straight from the horse's mouth—or rather from Johnnie Brandon's.

Tom Mackay saved Sir Herbert's little boy from drowning by swarming down the Gizzen Brae on his St. Kilda rope, and it was certainly a daring thing to do, though Tom won't admit it. Our Sir Herb. was very anxious to show some tangible token of his gratitude, but he was not at all sure how Tom Mackay would take it. Sir Herb. is gradually developing a sense of the fitness of things, and Tom Mackay is helping in the good work.

After much thought it was decided to donate a clock to the church, and as the scheme widened they found they had to add a tower, so that everyone would see the time. They decided to have a four-faced clock, but be it remembered that the tower and four faces were not in the original idea. It had leaked out that the Laird was to present a clock to the Glen, and Captain Reginald Mortimer-Jones, who thinks he owns the place, wanted the clock for the recreation hall. I suppose the deputation which went to the Lodge were thoroughly taken aback when they heard that clock and tower were to go on the kirk! Sir Herbert with his usual wish to 'ustle seemed to think that if he hurried, tower and clock would be ready for the New Year—and so they were! But *not* on the recreation hall! The deputation, I understand, are still licking their wounds.

If I write more I'll have to pay extra postage on this

air-mail letter, which would grieve my thrifty soul. Nookie's have a bit of trouble with a back tooth, and Sojer sympathizes with him to the extent of eating all the things Nookie can't eat.

There's midnight ringing out on the kirk clock—"and so to bed".

Ever your loving, longing wife,

Grizel.

From Kit Mackay to her folks in Edinburgh:

Kirk of the Corrie Manse,
Twelfth Night.

My dear people,

To-day came the glad news that the roads are clear at last! What a queer, unfamiliar, but *nice* festive season it has been. The Glen had a singular austere beauty and a silence which I confess fascinated me. The deer came stringing down from the heights, hungry and therefore tame. You could tell just by looking at the footprints in the snow that a lot of birds and beasts have been calling at the manse. We fed them all, and a queer wise-looking raven, who belongs to Seoras Gunn and answers to the name of Torquil, was a constant visitor until Seoras claimed him and took him home to Ravens Rock.

We have acquired, since I wrote you last, a most efficient and handy little helper. Yes, what I could never find in Edinburgh I have found in this Glen! "Explain?" you say. Grizel Gillespie, she likes me to use that name, found out that Mrs. Paterson had a little boarded-out lassie, and from what the lassie has told me she had been having a very hard time. Poor child, it was a bitter experience. But Mrs. Paterson did teach her how to turn out a room and scrub the kitchen table and floor. All the same she might have fed her better and seen that her garments fitted her. Everything that was sent her from headquarters was much too big. Mrs. P. was inclined at first to feel hurt that we had taken the girl, but she's now quite philosophic about it. She and her husband and brother can go out and in the kitchen much more freely now!

Now that we can all meet and exchange news in the Glen, the topic of conversation is the clock, and the new name for the church. We sat up on the last night of the year and listened with a good deal of emotion to the clock telling the hour of midnight and the beginning of the New Year. The clock had just chimed its last note when Stephen Mitchell and his choir struck up with, "Oh, God our help in ages past". It was wonderfully touching, and I was never so near "greeting" in the kirk as I was that night.

And who do you think preached our New Year sermon—the Doctor! He reached us with the help of a snow plough, a tractor and a land rover, and his own indomitable spirit.

He spoke of the forefolk in the Corrie, and the spirit of the past coming down to the present day. By the way, Tom had to file a lot of papers for the end of the year, and he put at the top of them all "The Kirk of the Corrie". When he mentioned it in the Presbytery, there was a burst of applause—the name was not only beautiful, it was historical. The Doctor said that he knew that in pre-Reformation times there had been a church in the Corrie, and by using the old name we were keeping alive an interesting piece of history. The tinkers seemed to have been the only ones who knew about it, and who were able after all these years to tell us the story.

Daisy and Tommy were sound asleep when we got home. At the manse door, Tom and I stood drinking in the beauty of the white silent world, and it seemed to me that the spirit of the old time had joined us that night and had rejoiced that there was no break between the long-gone past and the present. They and we are united in the Kirk of the Corrie.

And now I'll say A Happy New Year to you all,
With much love,
Kit.